Chapter 1

"Come on, Justin. We have to hurry home before Mom and Dad kill us."

Where is he? I have been walking through these woods behind our house for at least 5 minutes. The full moon was shining through the leaves on the trees above, giving me some light so I can see my way through. It is freezing outside, the cold wind nipping at my cheeks so I pulled my jacket closer around me. I continued to look around everywhere for Justin but I still couldn't find him. As I walked further in the woods, I never knew where I was. I was lost and I didn't like the feeling of it so I have to hurry and find Justin so I can hurry out of here. I keep calling Justin's name, but all I could hear was silence. It wasn't really quiet in the woods. As I was walking I can hear the owls hooting and the crickets chirping. Now I'm starting to get scared. I shouldn't have let Justin out of my sight. I paused and a chill ran up my spine as I heard a scream.

"Ebony!" I froze. That was Justin. He's in trouble. I start running toward the direction where I'm hearing Justin's screams. Sweat is beading up at my forehead and all I can think of is what could be possibly causing Justin to scream in such a horrifying way. I can't find him anywhere and now I'm very terrified. I stop at a pair of trees and it is now silent so I slowly walked behind the tree. I gasped by the grotesque scene that was right in front of me. I found Justin, but I was too late. Justin is lying on the ground, his neck shredded open, blood pouring out both the open wound and his mouth. I automatically broke down crying. And I had to keep myself from heaving so I had to keep it down but I can still taste it. That wasn't the only thing that has scared me. There was a wolf on top of him.

"No." I said under my breath but quickly covered my mouth, keeping in my cry but it was too late. The wolf looked up at me and

1

stared. Justin turned his head and blood was pouring out. He tried speaking.

"Ebony." He said, trying to reach out to me but I start backing away. The wolf got off of Justin and start walking towards me.

"Justin, I'll get help." After that, I start running. I was running as fast as I could as if my life depended on it. Well, my life did depend on it. The wolf could be chasing me. As I was running, I heard the howling of the wolf. That's when I woke up. My alarm clock was going off.

I sat up in the bed, trying to steady my heart beat. This nightmare has been happening for five years since I witnessed what happened to Justin. I was only12 and Justin was 7. When I left the woods, I told my mom and dad what happened. They automatically called the police and they searched for my brother's body but they couldn't find it. I knew right then that the wolf has taken it. My parents were so devastated that things had changed ever since. Justin's body was never found.

I reached over and hit the snooze button on my alarm clock. I put my hand up to my face and felt it was wet. I didn't even know I was crying but I'm not surprised. I really don't feel like going to school but really, I never felt like going to school. Next thing I know, there was a knock at my door.

"Ebony, it's time to get up. You have to get ready for school." I sighed.

"I'm already awake, mom." I got out of bed and went to my closet. I pulled out a gray rib tank top and some capris. I went to my bathroom and took a shower and brushed my teeth. After I got dressed, I went to my mirror to check myself out. My eyes were a little puffy from crying but I didn't care. I have pale skin with long, brown hair... well I used to have brown hair until I dyed it. Now it is black. My parents were so mad at me but I liked it so I kept it. I also have emerald green colored eyes. I decided to leave my hair out, framing my head. Many people said that with my hair framing my head, it make my eyes pop out but not literally. I put on a little mascara and went downstairs. By the time I got downstairs, my mom and dad was sitting at the table. My mom had fixed some pancakes, blueberry muffins, and strips of bacon. I grabbed a muffin and sat down. Dad put down his newspaper and looked at me.

"How was your night?"

"It was fine." I took bits and pieces of my muffin and ate it. I really wasn't that hungry. I checked my watch, took another bite out of my muffin and got up. My mom got up the same time.

"Bye sweetie." She gave me a hug and backed up. I grabbed my backpack by the door and left. This was our normal routine every day. It's been this way since Justin's death. I went to my blue Volkswagen bug that I got for my 16th birthday party. I got in the car and looked back towards the house before I drove off. My mom was standing in the doorway. As I drove off, my mom's figure got smaller and smaller.

I get to the school and found a parking spot. As usual, the parking lot is filled with students just getting to the school or they already been here, just hanging out with their friends. I sighed as I got out of my car. Here is another long day at school. I get in the building and go to my locker. My best friend, Jessica, was at her locker next to mine. Jessica and I have been friends since the first grade and now we are seniors. She is like a sister to me. She supported me while I grieved over Justin's horrible tragedy.

"Hey Ebony." I hugged Jessica before I opened up my locker.

"Hey Jessica." I pulled the locker door open and got out some textbooks. Jessica already had her locker opened. By her facial expression, I could already tell that she had something to tell me. She had a big smile on her face.

"Ebony, you can't believe what happened to me this weekend. You know Adam?"

"Yeah. He's the guy that lives next door to you that you keep talking about." We shut our lockers and start walking to our first class.

"He finally asked me out."

"Oh my gosh. Tell me what happened."

"It's a long story but all you need to know is that he finally found his feelings for me and now we are going on a date tomorrow." Jessica sound really excited. She then turned to me and smiled.

"Ebony, you need to get yourself a boyfriend." I sighed. She is always talking about this.

"You know why I don't want to date. Besides, I don't like any of these guys in this school." Many guys did ask me out but I turned them down. Either they were not my type or they were annoying or just immature.

"Come on. You only had one boyfriend and that was in the 3rd grade." Jessica was talking about Kyle. Kyle and I used to play, saying that we were married and we were really good friends but ever since middle school, he had changed. He tried fitting in with the popular people and he start getting annoying so we stopped being friends. As we were walking down the hallway, Jessica was still complaining, sharing her piece on how I need to start dating, but I wasn't paying attention because something caught my attention. This cute guy was walking down the hallway. He had black tousled hair and he had the bluest eyes I ever seen. He had high cheekbones, straight nose, and perfect lips. He didn't have a lot of muscles, but he looked lean and strong. I ran my fingers through my hair as I

4

watched him head to the guidance office. I felt my heart beat faster when he turned to look at me. I turned my head away fast as I felt myself blush. I feel so embarrassed. I can't believe that he caught me staring at him. He probably thought that I was weird. I turned back around and he was about to go into the guidance office. Before he went in, he turned to me and gave me a cute, crooked smile. After that, he went in.

"Hey Ebony! What is wrong with you?" I get out of my trance and look at Jessica. Jessica was looking at me like I was crazy.

"Are you okay?"

"Yeah. I'm fine." We got to our first period class, Chemistry. Jessica and I are partners so we sit next to each other.

"Alright." Jessica may say this right now, but I know she's still suspecting what happened. At least she would get off my back for now. As the bell rang, Ms. Brown got up from her desk. Ms. Brown looks like she is in her early 40s but she still looks young for her age.

"Okay class, today we will be doing an experiment." Before she got to say anymore, the cute boy from the hallway came in the class. Oh gosh. As soon as he entered into the classroom, he looked straight at me and smiled. I felt myself blush so I looked down. He didn't just catch my attention; he caught all the girls' attention, even Ms. Brown. He walked over to Ms. Brown and gave her a note.

"Okay class. We have a new student. His name is Logan." Jessica elbowed my side but I ignored her.

"Isn't he cute?" I continued to ignore her and looked back up. Ms. Brown starts talking again.

"Well Logan. Now I need to figure out where you sit." Ms. Brown starts looking around. All the other girls were pointing beside them, but I just looked away. Ms. Brown looked over to me.

"Jessica, your new seat is beside Amber in the back." Jessica sighed and got her stuff.

"I'll see you after class." Jessica whispered before she left. Ms. Brown turned to Logan.

"Logan you will sit next to Ebony. Ebony will be your lab partner all through the school year. Also she will show you around and help you out. Ebony, please raise your hand." I raised my hand slowly, but I still kept my head down. Next thing I know, Logan put his notebook on the table and sat down. With him sitting really close to me, it made me tense up. I looked up to Ms. Brown as she was beginning class. Even though I was looking forward, from the corner of my eye, I saw Logan looking at me. I tried my best to calm down and get my attention to Ms. Brown again but I couldn't help but to look over to him.

"Okay class, you will be working with your partners with this lab we are about to start. Pull out your lab books and turn to page 112." Everyone else in the class was getting their materials, starting out the experiment. I got up and went to get the materials. When I got back, I start setting up the materials but from the corner of my eye, I saw Logan was leaning against the lab table, looking at me. Some of his hair was in his face, making him look even cuter. I turned around and jumped when I saw how close he was.

"Umm, let us get started." I kept looking down to avoid his eyes.

"You don't have to get nervous around me. I won't bite." When he said that, he smiled, showing his nice, white teeth. I looked away and turned to the table.

"I'm not scared of you." I said while working on the experiment.

"You're sure about that." When he said this, he was getting closer to me.

"Why don't you show me what to do." he said as he stood there. Right now, I could feel Logan's eyes on me. It felt like daggers were digging in my back.

"Okay." I turned to him and start telling him what we will be doing. I demonstrated what to do. Logan was just watching me.

"Do you understand now?" I'm holding up the test tubes, showing him the reactions. Logan ran his fingers through his hair and pushed it back.

"I do." His eyes were focused on me. I looked towards the clock and just in time, the bell rang. I hurried up, gathering my stuff and left the classroom. I got down the hallway and Jessica stopped me.

"Ebony, slow down. You left out of the classroom so fast. What's wrong?"

"Nothing. I just don't want to be late for my next class."

"You almost left me. Don't you remember that we take the same second period?" I looked behind me to see if Logan was anywhere in sight. Jessica looked at me and smiled.

"It's that new guy, Logan, isn't it? I was looking at the both of you during class."

"I'm not running from him. I don't like him anyway."

"From the looks of it, it looked like he was flirting with you. I think he likes you."

"Whatever. Besides, there is something about him that seems mysterious."

"That's good."

"Shut up." I said while laughing. When Jessica and I start talking, someone tapped me on my shoulder. I turned around and jumped when I saw who it was. Logan was standing there. He looked to Jessica.

"Hey, what's your name?" It was like Jessica was hypnotized when Logan smiled at her.

"Jessica." When Jessica was saying this, she was playing with her golden locks of hair.

"Hey Jessica, do you mind if I talk to Ebony." I looked at Jessica, shaking my head no, but Jessica's attention was still on Logan.

"I don't mind." She turned to me.

"Ebony, I'll see you in class." After that, she went on to class. I turned to Logan and snarled and headed towards my locker. He has lost his mind, sending Jessica away.

I get to my locker and got my books for my next class. I shut the locker door and jumped when I saw Logan standing right there.

"What the... stop doing that. Why are you following me?" My heart is still beating fast from the scare.

"I told you, I need to talk to you about something important."

"Why don't you go mess with all the popular girls instead of messing with me?" His smile went right away.

"It seems like you don't want to cooperate with me."

"Nope." Before he got to say anymore, I ran to my next class. He just stood at my locker, watching me go to my next class.

Chapter 2

My next class is Trigonometry. By the time I got to class, the bell rang. I go to a seat next to Jessica.

"What took you so long? You were almost late for class."

"You think I don't know that. I had to get rid of Logan. You remember you left me with him." Jessica's face automatically lit up.

"What did he want to talk to you about?" After Jessica said that, Logan walked into the classroom. I sighed in frustration. The day can't get any worse. He gave Mr. Washington his schedule. While Mr. Washington was checking his attendance sheet, Logan looked at me and small, brief wave. Mr. Washington turned to the class.

"Okay class. We have a new student. Logan, you can sit anywhere you want." Of course when Mr. Washington said that, Logan went and sat in the seat on the other side of me. He gave me that same cute crooked smile he gave me in the hallway. Then, he leaned up and looked over at Jessica.

"Hey Jessica." Jessica, of course, smiled back.

"Hey Logan." Right after that, class started. Even though Mr. Washington was giving a lesson, I couldn't really pay attention. Logan was trying to get my attention. He kept tapping my arm. Finally, I lost it and I turned to him and gave him a sharp look. He passed me a note.

Before I was able to read it, someone came to my desk and took the note out of my hand. I looked up to see Mr. Washington standing there, frowning.

"Passing notes during class, I see." Mr. Washington turned to Logan.

"Young man, we do not pass notes during class." I looked at Logan and gave him a fake smile bit Mr. Washington was now looking at me and he frowned.

"And you, Ebony, should be ashamed of yourself." That is when Logan smiled at me. Mr. Washington is always strict so I was scared what the punishment would be. This is exactly why I'm always quiet in school, so I won't get in any trouble.

"Now for your punishment, both of you will get detention after school." I looked at Mr. Washington in shock.

"Detention?!? Mr. Washington, I didn't do anything. Logan was the one who passed the note." The other classmates start snickering and I felt myself blush of embarrassment. Mr. Washington just walked off and starts finishing up his lesson. I felt myself heat up with frustration. I looked at Logan and all I saw was red. Even though he didn't turn to me, I could tell he knew I was looking at him. I turned to Jessica. She had on her pity face. I turned back around. My parents will kill me when they find out that I have detention today. They probably wouldn't believe it because I never got in trouble. I was always a good student. I always got good grades. Ever since Logan got here, he starts ruining everything. For the rest of class, I just laid my head down. I really didn't care that I was doing that because I was already in trouble. When the bell rang, I just sat there a little while. Jessica got up and hugged me.

"At least your punishment wasn't something worse. You know how Mr. Washington can be." All I did was look at Jessica and gave her a hard glare and she looked away. I got up and went to my next class. Thank goodness Logan wasn't in any of my other classes because I don't know what I would have done if he was. When lunch time came, I didn't go. I just went to the library. I wasn't going to take any chances of running into HIM. When the end of the day came, I was almost eager to get home, but I remembered that I have to go to detention. Before I went to Mr. Washington's class, I went to my locker. Jessica was at her locker, packing up her stuff. I opened up my locker and got my stuff as Jessica shut hers and turned to me.

"I'll talk to you later." she said before hugging me good bye. We hugged and then I watched Jessica leave. I turned back around and frowned. This time I wasn't surprised. Logan was standing next to me.

"Are you stalking me? What part of leave me alone do you not understand?"

"First of all, I'm not stalking you. I bet you wished that I was stalking you, though. Second, I'm just going to my locker."

"What locker?" Logan smiled at me and went to the locker right beside mines and start opening it up.

"You did this on purpose. You just love messing with me. This is your first day and you're already messing things up for me."

"I don't know what you're talking about." Logan tried to sound innocent.

"Whatever." I start walking away, but Logan grabbed my arm. I looked around to see if anyone was around. The hallway was empty. Logan pulled me close. I looked up into his blue eyes.

"Get off of me or I will scream..." Before I got to say anything else, Logan kissed me. I felt sparks as soon as he kissed me. I was so shocked, I didn't react. Next thing I know, I'm kissing him back. His lips are so soft. I started to feel a little weird inside, but weird in a good way. I wrapped my arms around his neck as he pulled me in closer. As things were getting good and I still didn't realize what I was doing, I heard someone clear their voice. I quickly pushed Logan away and turned to see Mr. Washington standing a few feet away from us, with a frown on his face. Not again!!! This is too embarrassing.

"First, I catch the both of you passing notes. Now I find the both of you in the hallway kissing." I was about to say something, but I stopped. I felt myself blush of embarrassment. I looked over to Logan to see his expression. Logan was just looking at Mr. Washington, with no expression on his face, like he didn't care what was happening right now. I bet he didn't pay attention to any word that Mr. Washington said. I turned back to Mr. Washington.

"Mr. Washington, I'm sorry..." Before I got to say anything else, Mr. Washington interrupted.

"Just go to my classroom." After he said that very sternly, he stormed away. I turned to Logan and frowned.

"See, look what you done. You just got me in trouble again with the same teacher. If you haven't kissed me, none of this would have happened." I didn't even let him reply. I just walked off without turning back.

Chapter 3

I can't believe this. I feel so embarrassed after being caught kissing that jerk. I should have pushed him away as soon as he kissed me. What is wrong with me... no, what's wrong with Logan. Why out of all the popular and pretty girls, he comes messing with me. I know I wasn't bringing him on because I never said anything to him, nor was I flirting with him. Also, he keeps claiming that he has something to tell me, but I keep ignoring him. Logan seemed so eager to tell me what he had to say, which kind of caused me to get more eager to find out. All I know is that I have to take my focus off of this and put my focus on getting through detention. I get to Mr. Washington's class and I'm the only one in here. I sit in one of the seats in the front and took out some of my homework so I can do it. As I was doing my work, I heard some noises in the hallway. I get up and looked in the hallway to see if anyone was coming, but I didn't see anyone. When I turned back around, Logan was standing right behind me.

"How did you get in .... Never mind. I don't even care anymore." I went back to my seat and sat down. I watched as Logan walked from the door to the seat next to me. I took out my notebook and start doodling. The thing is that I don't know what I'm drawing because my mind is on how my life has gone upside down in a day because of Logan. He has ruined everything because of what he wanted to tell me. He has also embarrassed me in front of Mr. Washington. I looked down at my notebook and wasn't surprised when I saw a drawing of me strangling Logan. I drew Logan with big eyes as he was suffocating. I tore the paper out my notebook, balled it up and threw it towards the trash can. I was hoping that it was going to make it in the trash can, but it missed instead. Mr. Washington came in the classroom and frowned at me.

"I am so surprised of your behavior today, Ebony. Go pick up that paper ball." I blushed with embarrassment as I followed Mr.

Washington's orders. As I was sitting in my seat, I watched as Logan start snickering. I sighed in frustration. This is going to be a long detention. All we did was stay in our seats and watched the clock. At least, that is what I did. As soon as the clock went to 5 o' clock, I was the first one out of the door. I got in my car and drove off. I didn't even bother looking back.

Chapter 4

I parked my car in the garage and walked towards the front door.

"Hey Ebony." I turned to see my next door neighbor, Randy, standing behind me. He is one of the popular guys in school. When we are in school, we don't talk to each other since I really don't talk in school. But as soon as we get home, he's all nice to me and he talks to me.

"Hey Randy." I take my keys out and start unlocking the door. I know Randy could already tell that I was upset.

"What's wrong?" He looked concerned but I really didn't feel like talking to Randy today.

"I'm sorry Randy. I just had a stressful day and I just don't feel like talking about it. Can we just talk later?" At first, I thought he looked disappointed but it went away so quickly that I wasn't sure.

"Okay. Just call me when you feel like talking."

"Thanks." When I opened the door and walked in, Randy walked across the street to his house. I shut the door and I hear my mother laugh. I was kind of surprised because my mom barely laughs anymore. Her voice was coming from the kitchen. It sounds like she was talking to someone so I walked toward the kitchen.

"Mom, you can't believe what had happened today..." Before I got to finish, I saw my mom sitting at the kitchen table, talking to the guy who I really despise right now... Logan. Both of them looked up, mom smiling at me and Logan giving me a smile too.

"Hey Ebony, this is Logan. He and his family just moved in the house next door. It turns out that he goes to your school." I didn't even say anything. I just looked at him with hatred. My mother looked from me and Logan and her smile went away.

15

"I'm guessing you guys have already met."

"Unfortunately, yes. Logan, you want to tell my mom what happened today or should I." I said as I gave him a fake smile.

"Go ahead. I don't mind." He looked so calm.

"Well, Logan is the reason why I'm late. That idiot... that big jerk..." I felt my pressure going up and I was getting so angry. I noticed that I was raising my voice at Logan.

"Calm down Ebony. And don't talk bad about Logan. I did not raise you to act like this. I am so ashamed of you." she turned to Logan.

"I'm so sorry, Logan. I do not know what is wrong with Ebony. She is never like that."

"But mom, he caused me to get..."

"No Ebony. I don't care. You better apologize to Logan." Logan got up and smiled at me. I sighed and put a fake smile on my face.

"I'm sorry." I said under my breath. Logan smiled at me.

"It's okay." He turned to my mom.

"Thank you Mrs. Jenkins for the chat but I have to go."

"Thank you for coming." Mom gave him a smile.

"I'll walk you out." We start walking toward the door.

When we got to the door, which is out of hearing distance of my mom, I opened the door and stood to the side and my smile went away real fast. Logan stood in front of me.

"How dare you come to my house? Are you stalking me? You already messed things up for me at school." I whispered. I turned around to make sure my mom wasn't there.

"I don't know what you are talking about?" He gave me the same innocent look he gave me earlier.

"I want you to leave me alone. Don't you ever come to my house ever again. Just stay out of my life."

"That is going to cost you something."

"Cost what?" He starts moving closer to me. He looked down at me and gave me his sexy smile.

"I want a kiss like the one from earlier."

"Oh you want a kiss." I said flirtatiously. I moved closer and put a hand on his chest. I looked up in his eyes.

"Yeah." I leaned closer and got on my tippy toes and whispered in his ear.

"I got something better." After I said that, I kneed him in his special manly place. He bent over and groaned.

"How to you like that? Now leave me alone." After that, I pushed him out the house and shut the door in his face. After that, I ran upstairs to my room. I am so pissed right now. Why am I letting this... this JERK get me so angry. I need to call Jessica. I sat on my bed and took out my cell phone and called Jessica. She answered after three rings.

"Hello."

"Hey Jessica."

"Hey Ebony. You sound stressed out."

"You know how my day was bad all during school? It got so worse afterwards."

"Tell me what happened." I told Jessica about what happened after school. I told her about how Logan kissed me and how he now live next door to me. I also mentioned how he came to my house and embarrassed me in front of my mom.

"Isn't that crazy? I just want to punch him in his face because he is so annoying." At first it was quiet on the other end, but Jessica finally said something.

"OMG!!! He kissed you!" Jessica sounded so excited.

"That's all you heard. He has been stalking me all day and he took advantage of me, but all you're thinking about is that he kissed me." Even when I said that, she ignored it.

"Did you like it? How was it?"

"Bye Jessica. I have to go. I'll talk to you later." I felt my face heating up from anger and I didn't want to yell at her.

"I'm sorry Ebony. Everything will be alright. Just calm down and don't let Logan get to you...Well..."

"Well what." I snapped.

"Maybe you like him."

"No. Why would you say that? Why would I like him?" I felt myself blush.

"You have some feelings for him since you letting him get you this angry."

"Angry! You said I'm angry! I'm not angry, just a little upset." I'm shocked that Jessica even said that.

18

"Yeah. Okay. Just think about what I said. I got to go."

"Okay. Talk to you later. Bye."

"Bye." Jessica said before she hung up. I actually start thinking about what Jessica said. Why am I letting him get to me? This is probably what he wanted, him being stuck in my head, getting me angry. All I need to do is get my mind off of him and I will be alright. I took out my homework and did it. After I finished, mom came upstairs to my room.

"Ebony, your father is here and dinner is ready."

"Okay, I'm coming down." I went downstairs to the dining room and mom already had dinner set out. We are having spaghetti and meatballs with salad on the side. Dad was already sitting at the head of the table. My dad is a lawyer and sometimes he come home early, like today, or he wouldn't come home until like 10 or 11 o'clock pm. Mom sat right next to him and I sat on the other side. When we start eating, like usual, dinner was quiet. There was no "hello." or "how was your day?" or anything else. All we did was eat dinner quietly. After we finished, my dad went to his office and mom went to wash the dishes while I went back to my room. Right now, it was 8:30 pm. That was when I remembered about Randy and how I'm supposed to be calling him but I still didn't feel like talking to him. I am just tired and exhausted, so I got ready for bed. I took a shower and put on some shorts and a tank top as my PJs and went to bed, As soon as my head hit the pillow, I fell asleep... without thinking about Logan.

Chapter 5

I wake up and all I see is darkness. I looked around and noticed that I wasn't in my room. I saw that I was in the woods again. I got up from the ground and looked up. A few feet away there was a small figure standing there. I couldn't see what it was at first because of the fog, but it drifted away. My heart skipped a beat when I saw it was Justin who was standing in front of me.

"Justin!" I yelled. I ran to him, dropped on my knees and hugged him. As soon as I hugged his small, fragile body, I start crying even harder.

"You're alive. I missed you so much." I said. All of a sudden, I hear Justin trying to say something.

""He did this." Justin whimpered.

"What?" At first I didn't hear him.

"He did this to me." I stepped back and looked down at Justin's sweet face. His brown hair was damp and his face was wet from tears. I got up.

"Who did what to you?" I asked.

"He did this to me." Justin said again.

"Who Justin?" After that a dark figure stepped behind him and put its hands on Justin's shoulder.

"I can't tell." Justin said. He looked so frightened. After that, both of them disappeared.

"No, Justin. Who?" I yelled. After that, I start running.

"Justin...Justin..." I kept running. My chest starts to burn from being out of breath. That's when the howling started. The same howling of the wolf that I heard the night Justin died.

That is when I woke up. My heart is beating so fast. After my heart calmed down, I start crying. That was the worst dream I ever had. What was Justin talking about when he said that he did it? Who is HE? I am just stressed out. When I finally calmed down, I heard it again. Am I still dreaming? I pinched myself and from the yelp that came out of my mouth and the pain I felt, it showed that I wasn't dreaming. I listened closely and I am most positive that I did hear what I thought I heard... the howl. My heart starts beating real fast. A part of me wants to go out and check on it, but the other part of me is telling me to stay here. I know my answer so I got up and put on some sweats and my hoodie. I went downstairs and went out the back door in the kitchen, which leads to the woods where I heard the howl. Before I left, I grabbed a flashlight.

I start walking my way through the woods, the light from the flashlight helping me. As I was walking through here, I was feeling so many emotions that I felt the last time I was in here five years ago. The howling kept going, but after a few minutes, it stopped. It was like it could sense that I was there and that is when I stopped walking. I start getting scared and shivers were going down my spine. After a while, I start hearing rustles from the leaves. It was coming from behind me. My heart start racing as I turned around.

Who's out there?" I start getting alert. No one answered, so I kept walking toward where I heard the rustling.

Who's out there?" I asked again. All of a sudden, someone grabbed me from behind and covered my mouth before I got to scream. The person turned me around and I saw it was Logan. Now I'm mad.

"If I uncover your mouth, would you keep quiet?" He asked. I shook my head yes. He looked at me suspiciously for a minute, but he finally uncovered my mouth. I gave him a smile, but then kneed him in his special manly place again. He bent over and groaned.

"What the???... are you crazy?!?!" He yelled at me.

"No. You the one who decided to grab me." I yelled back.

"Well excuse me. Next time I see a girl walking alone in dangerous woods, I would just leave her there and let whatever happens to her happens." He straightened up. I could tell he was getting real angry, but he took a deep breath and calmed down.

"What are you doing in here anyway? It's so dark out here; you don't know what could happen." He asked.

"It's none of your business. Besides, what are YOU doing out here?"

"You answer me first?"

"Fine. I heard something and I wanted to check things out." I said.

"Alone?"

"Yes. I can take care of myself." I snapped.

"You can?" He start moving closer to me. I swallowed hard.

"Yes..." I said as I stepped back a little. A smirk came to his face as he saw I was nervous.

"From anything?" Now he is right in front of me. My heart starts racing again.

"Yes...and anyone." I stuttered. He laughed a little.

"Now tell me why it is so hard to believe that."

"It's true." I snapped.

"Then why are you so nervous?"

"I'm not scared of you." I said.

"I never said you were." He brushed a strand of hair out of my face. My heart start beating faster as his blue eyes gazed into my eyes. He's right. He does scare me, but in a certain way. There is something mysterious about him that screams danger and mystery, but I can't help the fact that he still grabs my attention.

All of a sudden, I noticed that Logan didn't have a shirt on, so he was bare chest. He had a long, thin scar on the right side of his chest. It looks so unusual, I wonder what happened. Before I knew it, I'm touching his chest where the scar is. His skin is so warm. I felt him tense up, but he relaxed. I looked back up into his eyes. That is when I heard rustle of leaves of someone coming. I could tell Logan heard it too because he looked alert. He looked back down at me.

"I..." Before he got to say anything, I hear a familiar voice call my name.

"Ebony." I turned around and Randy comes forward from the tree.

"Randy, what you doing here?"

"I saw you walking in here. Who were you talking to?" he asked.

"I..." I turned around and saw that Logan was gone.

"No one. I was talking to no one." I said. Randy looked confused, but it went away. I bet he thinks I'm weird now. I feel embarrassed.

"Well, what you doing out here?"

"I was going for a nice walk." I lied. I gave him a fake smile.

"At 1 o' clock in the morning?... Never mind. Let me walk you home."

"I'm fine Randy... fine." I did not want to start any debate because I knew Randy wouldn't leave it alone until I said okay. He took off his jacket and wrapped it around me and we start walking back to my house. I looked behind me one last time to where Logan stood. Where did he go?

Chapter 6

I couldn't sleep for the rest of the night. All I could think about was, unfortunately, Logan. Last night, when we talked and that moment we had, I felt a connection. It was so weird because I never felt anything like this before. It was like we were in our own little world as soon as I looked him in his eyes. Everything was calm, but then Randy came and Logan left. I don't know where he went or how he left so quickly without getting caught by Randy. That is what brings more mystery to Logan. I never really noticed that I forgot about the wolf howls I heard last night. When Randy walked me back home, thank goodness mom and dad was still asleep. All I did was say thank you to Randy and we went our separate ways. I got back in bed, but I couldn't fall back to sleep. Now it is morning and my alarm clock went off on the scheduled time. I yawned and got out of bed. I took a shower and put on some skinny jeans and a lime green tank top with a light blue jean jacket. I didn't feel like messing with my hair so I put it into a ponytail. After I was done, I went downstairs and mom and dad was sitting at the table. I went to the fridge and took me out a bottle of apple juice.

"Ebony, you need to eat something. You look exhausted." mom said. Of course since I didn't get any sleep last night.

"I'm not hungry."

"Ebony, listen to your mother." Dad said. He wasn't even paying attention. He was too busy reading the newspaper. I didn't want to argue so I grabbed an apple from the bowl on the table, rinsed it off and took a bite.

"Happy now?"

"Yes." Mom smiled.

"Good. I'm leaving now." I grabbed my keys from the hook on the wall.

"Wait, I almost forgot. Someone needs a ride to school." mom said.

"Okay, I'll drive Randy to school." I said. Then, mom starts looking uncomfortable.

"What mom?"

"I wasn't talking about Randy." When she said that, there was a knock at the door. I knew right away who she was talking about.

"No. You didn't mean... No, you're kidding right?"

"Calm down Ebony. You are embarrassing yourself." mom said as she left the kitchen. I hear her opening up the door.

"Hello Logan. How are you?" mom said in her cheerful voice. Dad finally looked up from his newspaper and looked at me. He looked so confused.

"Wait, what is going on? Who is Logan?" I rolled my eyes. Dad really needs to be home more often.

"He's our new next door neighbor." I mumbled. Mom and Logan came into the kitchen. As soon as Logan comes in, he looks at me with a small smile on his face. I know he is enjoying this, torturing me.

Dad got up, a hard look on his face.

"So this is Logan?" He asked.

"Yes. He and his family just moved into the house next door." mom said. Dad face softened. No dad, look mean again. Then Logan will know to leave me alone. Then I just noticed that Logan is a little taller than dad, and dad is tall. Also, Logan does look like one of those fighting types so he might beat my dad in a fight, so there is no use.

"Hello sir."

"Have a safe drive to school." Dad hugged me and sat back down. I grabbed my backpack and walked out while Logan followed me. I walked out of the house to the garage and got in the car. I didn't say anything to him. Logan got in and as soon as he shut the door, I let everything out.

"You are full of it, you know that." I snapped at him. He looked taken back, as if he wasn't expecting that.

"What did I do now?"

"You already know. Going to my mom about getting a ride. What happened to your car?"

"It's acting up." He said. I just sighed and started the car. After that, I drove off.

I glanced over at Logan. He was looking out of the window. I felt my face heat up as Logan looked at my direction.

"You can take a picture if you want. I don't mind." He said.

"I don't know what you talking about." Man, he caught me. I feel so embarrassed.

"You don't have to hide it. I know you're into me. You showed it last night."

"Whatever. You can think that all you want. Have fantasies or whatever" I pulled up to the school and parked in the parking lot. I got out the car and Logan got out. When I locked the car, I turned around and jumped when I saw Logan was standing there. He smiled at me.

"Can you stop doing that?" I said in frustration. I tried walking past him, but he didn't move.

"Excuse me." He didn't even move out of my way. All he did was get closer. I looked around to see if anyone was watching.

"So you're not into me?" He asked low enough for only me to hear.

"N..no." I stammered. That made Logan's smile broaden even more. Why didn't I keep my voice in control?

"You are a bad liar."

"And you are a jack..." He placed a finger on my lips to stop me.

"You have a dirty mouth."

"Move out of my way Logan."

"Why don't you make me?" He starts leaning his face toward mine. My heart was beating so fast. A part of me wanted this kiss, but he is such a jerk and if it happens, he would count that as he is right. When our lips almost touched, I hear Jessica's voice.

"Ebony?" Logan stepped back. I was filled with relief. Thank you God I was saved.

"Hey Jessica." I said to her cheerfully.

"Hey Ebony. Did I interrupt something?" She had a huge smile on her face.

"No. I was just about to walk into the school. So was Logan." Jessica turned to Logan.

"Hey Logan." Jessica said.

"Hey. I guess I will see you girls later. Especially you Ebony." He smiled at me before he left. As I watched as Logan leave, I turned around and saw Jessica still smiling.

"What?" I start walking toward the school. Jessica caught up with me.

"You know what. What was that back there?"

"Nothing."

"Yeah. It could have been something if I didn't interrupt." Jessica said.

"Which I thank you, by the way. You saved me."

"Ebony, you know you wanted it to happen."

"No I didn't"

"I know you. You wanted that kiss and you are attracted to Logan and he's attracted to you." That last part got my attention.

"He is not attracted to me. I think he is all about fun and games. He's just messing with me."

"I can tell he likes you. He could go to any other girl out of the open girls in our school."

"Whatever." I just wanted to change the subject. We walked into the school and went to our lockers.

"So, aren't you excited about your date tomorrow on Wednesday?"

"Yes! I can't wait until tomorrow. Adam called me today. He will be sitting with us today at lunch. He told me it's a surprise to where we going tomorrow." Jessica said. She is so excited. The five minute bell rang. I got my books out of my locker and put my backpack in there and shut it. We start walking to our classes. I have physical education and Jessica has Art.

"I'll talk to you later." Jessica said as she went to her class.

I get to gym and go to the girls' locker room. I went to my locker and got out my gym clothes, a gray tank top and some shorts. I'm mad because I'm alone in this class since Jessica is not in here. All the other girls talk to their friends while I just stay quiet. The boys pay attention to me, but in their pervish ways. Either way, I'm still lonely.

After fixing my ponytail, I walked out into the gym where the other students were. I sat on the bench waiting for class to start. Next thing I know, someone sits next to me.

"Hey. We need to stop meeting like this." The person said. Right away, I knew who it was. I rolled my eyes as I looked beside me to see Logan sitting there, smiling.

"What are you doing here?" I hissed at him.

"I'm in this class." God, why me? Why are you doing this to me, letting this jerk be in most of my classes.

"You have to switch out. I don't want you to be here. "

"Too bad because I want to be here." He said. I sighed.

"Fine. But, don't talk to me or anything."

"Why? You look like you could use some company."

"I like being alone."

"Yeah, okay. I don't believe you." He said. Before I got to say anything, Coach Carter came out. She is so strong; I would think that she used to be a man.

"Hello class. We have a new student. Logan, can you stand up?" Logan just raised his hand, not following Ms. Carter's orders. Now he is going to be on her bad side by the look on her face.

"Okay class, today you guys will be working on your archery skills. Grab your bows and arrows and grab a partner." Automatically, Claire, one of the popular girls in school, comes over. Claire is so snobbish, but she is lucky she is pretty with her blonde hair and pretty face.

"Hey Logan. I could use a partner. Can you be my partner?" She said flirtatiously as she played with her hair. I rolled my eyes as I hear her say this fake line. Claire pretends to be sweet, but no one likes her really.

"No thanks. Ebony is my partner." He said as he put his arm around me.

"Wait, what?!?" She said. She looked just as surprised as I am.

"Ebony's my partner."

"So you're choosing her over this." She points to herself.

"Yes." he said simply.

"Fine." She gave me a dirty look and walked away. I turned to Logan.

"Do you know you just said no to one of the most popular and hottest girls in the school?" All Logan did was shrug his shoulder.

"I don't care. Now let's go." He got up and started walking away, but he stopped when he saw I wasn't following him outside.

"Come on." he said.

"You didn't even ask me to be your partner." he sighed and walked back.

"Can you be my partner?"

"Fine. It's not like I have anyone else to choose from." I got up and we walked out of the building to the field where everyone else is. We got our bows and arrows from the box and got in front of a target board. I hate this sport because I'm not so good at it.

"You want to go first?" he asked.

"No. You can go." We stood at least 12 feet from the board. He got the bow and arrow in position. I couldn't help to watch as Logan focused on the board, the muscle in his arm flex as he prepares the position. When he let go, the arrow went flying and it hit the board. I walked over to the board and was surprised that the arrow hit straight in the middle, bull's-eye. I tried pulling it out, but it was in so deep. That was a strong strike.

"A little help would be nice." I yelled to Logan. He starts laughing as he walks up to me. I step aside as he pull the arrow out easily. Either he is so strong or I'm just weak. We walked back to the spot.

"I'm not so good at this, just to let you know." I said as I try to get in position.

"Just try your best. You can't be that bad." I let go and the arrow didn't even make it halfway near the board. I felt so embarrassed; I felt my face turning red. I turned to Logan and saw he was trying to keep himself from laughing.

"That was not funny. That was horrible." Logan went and picked up the arrow.

"It's okay. Not everyone is good at some things. Let me help you." He got behind me and he was so close, I could feel goosebumps forming on my arms.

"Now get into the right position." he said. I followed his order as I got into the position. Next thing he does is grab my arms as he put them in the right position.

"There. Now let go." He said in my ear. I did and the arrow went flying until it hit the board. I was so excited.

"Oh my gosh. It hit the board for the first time." I squealed as I jumped up and down like a kid.

"Thank you so much." I said as I turned around and hugged him. He seemed to be shocked at first, but he hugged me back. After a while, I just noticed what I was doing so I stepped back.

"Umm… well thanks for the help." I didn't even look him in his face.

"Ebony..." Logan start to say, but I stopped him.

"Let's just finish practicing." I felt so awkward. I looked around to see if anyone was watching, but everyone was too busy practicing with their partner. For the rest of practice, we didn't even say anything to each other. Logan helped me a little more, but that's it.

"Time is up. Hit the locker rooms." Ms. Carter yelled. As soon as she said that, I ran off, leaving Logan behind.

"I enter the locker room and all the girls get quiet, all their eyes on me. I feel myself blush as I walked to my locker. I'm not used to all

34

this attention I am getting. As I was putting on my clothes, I hear the girls whispering. I could feel all their eyes on me. When I turned around to leave, Claire and her posse are standing there.

"Excuse me." I said as I tried to walk past, but Claire got in my way.

"So little quiet Ebony thinks she's all special because the new boy choose her to be his partner." Claire sneered.

"I need to get to class."

"What's the rush? You need to run to Logan."

"Claire, you need to move." All she did was ignore me. I am getting so angry right now.

"Aww look girls, Ebony's mad." Finally, I just lost it and I pushed her aside.

"I said move." I knew her posse wouldn't do anything because all they care about is their looks. Claire got mad so she pushed me back.

"No. What are you going to do about it?" That's when I grabbed her hair and start hitting her with all my strength.

"Get off, crazy!!!" Claire yelled. That's when I got back to my senses and I back off. Claire straightened up and I saw that her lip was bleeding. She seemed to feel it because she touched her lip and looked at the blood that was on her finger.

"OMG!!! I'm bleeding!!!" That's when she fainted. All the girls gasped and looked at me. I defeated the wicked witch basically. They all moved out of my way as I walked out of the room. "Just calm down, Ebony. Calm down." I kept saying to myself. I couldn't calm down, but I still went to my next class, AP Calculus. I get in and see Jessica is already in there. She was smiling, but her smile went away as soon as she saw my face.

"What's wrong, Ebony? Is Logan in another one of your classes again? And what happened to your hair?"

"Yeah, Logan is in my PE class, but that is not why I'm pissed. Claire is now on me because Logan chose to be my partner instead of hers when she asked." I said as I took my hair out of the ponytail and ran my fingers through it.

"Wait...Did you just say that someone turned down Claire?" Jessica looked so shocked.

"Yeah. That's how I reacted too. Her and her posse tried to gang up on me, but I showed her. She is now unconscious on the locker room floor."

"You knocked her out?" Jessica asked as her eyes got all wide.

"No, she fainted when I scratched her lip and it starts bleeding, but she deserved it." Jessica giggled when I said this, causing me to giggle too. I looked at the clock. Please may it ring.

"What's wrong now?" Jessica asked.

"Oh. I just want to make sure that Logan doesn't have this class too."

"Calm down, Ebony. You have nothing to worry about."

"You're right." Ms. Robinson, our teacher, was standing at the door. Yes! No Logan in this class, I thought cheerfully. I'm starting to feel much better. That's when a hand pushed the door open. I've spoken too soon.

Chapter 7

"Sorry, I almost got lost. I'm the new student." Logan comes into the classroom. At least there was someone already sitting in the seat beside me. So you know what he does? He sits in the seat behind me. I know he is going to take any chance he could to mess with me. While Ms. Robinson was giving the lesson, I couldn't concentrate. Something wasn't feeling right. Something was telling me to look towards the door. The sound of Ms. Robinson's voice was fading away. That's when the scream came. Everyone looked towards the window where we heard the scream.

"What the hell was that?" Jessica said. Everyone ran out of the room. I got up and start to follow, but Jessica called me.

"Ebony, what are you doing?" she asked.

"I'm going to check it out. Let's see what's going on." At first, Jessica seemed hesitant, but she got up.

"I'll come with you." Logan said. This is the most serious I have seen him. We went outside to where the crowd is. People were whispering and gasping. All of a sudden, there was this voice in my head telling me to get closer. I start pushing through the crowd. I could hear Jessica behind me saying,

"What is she doing?" I get to the front and I see a little girl. She looks so terrified. One of the administrators tried calming her down, but she wouldn't let any of them touch her. She looked no older than 5. She looks so adorable with her straight brown hair and her blue eyes. It was like she knew I was looking at her because she looked right at me and she ran to me and hugged my legs. She looked up at me with her big blue eyes.

"He knows you're still alive." She says. This is so confusing.

"Wait, what?"

"Do you know this little girl?" asked the administrator.

"Uh... Yeah. She's... my little sister." I lied. The administrator looked at me for a little while, but then he turned away.

"There is nothing to see here. Everyone go back inside." he said before he turned back to me.

"Handle this." The administrator said before he walked inside the school with the others. Jessica and Logan walked up to us.

"Ebony, why didn't you tell me you have a sister. Is she adopted?" Jessica asked, smiling at the little girl.

"I lied. She's trying to tell me something. Little girl, what is your name?"

"He knows you alive." the girl repeated, ignoring my question.

"Who know I'm still alive?"

"He's coming. In three days on the full moon, war begins. You dead." she said. That's when chills went down my spine. What she mean war? Why am I going to die? This makes no sense. The girl continues to talk.

"He failed the first time, but he will succeed."

"What are you talking about?" The girl looked past me and pointed behind me.

"Ask him." she whispers. I looked behind me and see she's pointing to Logan.

"Wait...what?" I turned back around and the girl is gone.

"This is some scary stuff." Jessica said.

"What does she mean he knows I'm alive?"

"Can we go inside now?" Jessica whined, but I didn't pay attention to her. I turned to Logan who was quiet. His face was pale, as if he just saw a ghost. I start thinking about this. I just remembered today is the anniversary of Justin's death. But what does Logan have to do with any of this?

"Ebony?" Jessica shook me.

"Oh sorry. Yes?"

"Can we go inside?"

"No. We can't. I'm too late." Logan says.

"What are you talking about?" I asked.

"We have to go. I'll tell you when we get in the car."

"Well, you guys enjoy each other's company. I'll just go inside..." Jessica said as she starts backing away to the school.

"You can't leave. You're in this now since you heard what the girl said."

"I didn't hear anything. I won't tell anyone, I promise."

"Sorry, you're in danger now. They are watching us right now. If you stay, they will find you and you will die."

"Who are 'they'? This is too confusing. Why do we have to leave?" I asked.

"Just go to your locker, both of you, and get what you need. Meet me at the car." After that, he ran off. Jessica and I turned to each other and start walking towards the school.

"I need to get my backpack from my locker because my purse and keys are in there." Jessica looked at me like I was crazy.

"Are you serious? That little girl just told you about there being a war and all that stuff. I can't stay because now I'm not safe. Yet, you're talking about what you need. Am I the only confused person here?" Jessica said.

"I'm as confused as you are. We just have to wait until Logan tells us what's going on." We get to our locker and get our stuff. All of a sudden, it seems like it have gotten cold in here. Then I hear a whoosh, as if someone just walked past us.

"Did you hear that?"

"That's the problem. I'm hearing too much. This is what got me in this situation in the first place." Jessica snapped.

"No, not that. Someone is in this hallway with us." We kept quiet as we listened.

"I don't hear anything. Let's just leave before your boyfriend comes and try to find us."

"Logan is not my boyfriend."

"Yeah. Okay." We get our stuff and leave our lockers.

As we walked through the hallway, this man who look like those bad men in the movies, with his slick back hair, dark sunglasses, leather jacket, and his clothes are black. He is very huge and muscled. Something was telling me that something bad was about to happen so Jessica and I turned to walk the other way, but a guy who was dressed like the other guy was walking down the other way. We were trapped.

"Um, Ebony... You know those men?" Jessica asked nervously.

"No. You?"

"Nope. That is why I asked you/"

"Well, I don't know them."

"Maybe they are aliens."

"Aliens?"

"Yeah." Jessica took a step toward them.

"Welcome to America." Jessica said slowly and loud. I swear this is one of Jessica's dumb blonde moments. One of the guys raised an eyebrow at Jessica.

"Jessica. Maybe we should leave."

"Not yet. Maybe they are still trying to understand."

"Jessica..."

"We... are... humans. Why did you come to our planet? This is earth." I rolled my eyes.

"Jessica, you are embarrassing yourself."

"No I'm not. This is awesome."

"I don't think they are aliens. You can basically see that they understand you."

"Thank god. I thought I would have to talk like that forever."

"Yeah.... Let's leave.... now." That's when both of the men start walking closer from each side.

"Ebony, something is telling me that they are bad people." Jessica said frightened. I gave her the "you think" look. There were no more hallways and the only way we could escape is through the window in front of us, but we can't break the glass because we are not strong enough. All of a sudden, someone jumps through that window and landed on his one of his knees. When he got up, I see its Logan. That's when the two men were close enough that they start to attack Logan.

"Logan!" I screamed. There was no way that Logan can beat both of those huge men. The men were giving punches, but Logan blocked them. The first man start running toward Logan, but Logan jumped up and kicked the guy in the chest. It must have been a powerful kick because the man was sent flying across the hallway against the wall. No, not against the wall- IN the wall. What is he? Superman?

Logan turned to us.

"Go. Go to the car now. I'll meet you there."

"What the hell was that?" I asked. I'm still shocked.

"Go!!" Logan yelled as he ducked as the second man swung at him. Swiftly, Logan turned around and all I hear is a wet, snapping sound of something breaking. The guy fell on the ground, his head in an awkward position, blood pouring out of his mouth. Logan just broke the man's neck.

"You don't have to tell me twice! Come on Ebony!" Jessica yelled as she stepped out of the window and she start running towards the parking lot. I looked back at Logan before I start running too. "What is he?" kept playing over and over in my mind.

Chapter 8

We got in the car, Jessica getting in the back and me getting in the driver's side. I look up to see a black SUV in front of the school, facing us. I'm trying to turn on the car as I see the door open and three men dressed like the men inside the school get out. They start running towards us.

"There are more of them?"

"I don't care. All I want you to do is drive away." Jessica yelled.

"I can't."

"Why the hell not?"

"My car won't start."

"You and your stupid car."

"Hey! I didn't buy the car. Dad did. So why don't you blame him." Jessica was about to say something, but she ended up screaming when one of the men punched his fist through the window and tried to grab for me. I climbed to the back of the seat and stayed close to Jessica. The next thing I know, the man tore off the door to my car and threw it across the street. They smiled.

"Oh my God Ebony. We are going to die. I might as well tell you that I accidently dropped your earphones in dog poop last week."

"What! I have been using it and now you tell me!"

"Sorry. I cleaned it off." she said. I was about to say something else, but one of the guys grabbed my ankle and pulled me out of the car. I tried to kick the guy off me, but he just dragged me out of the car. I was screaming to the top of my lungs, hoping someone would hear me. He picked me up and tried to take me to the SUV, but Logan stopped him and pulled me away from him. The guy grabbed

Logan's throat, but Logan punched his fist through the man's chest. The man let go of Logan's neck and fell to his knees. Logan pulled out the man's heart and the guy just went limp to the ground. I stared at Logan in horror. He turned to me and his eyes were glowing and his hands were bloody, with the heart still in one of them, still beating. He dropped the heart as his eyes went back to normal.

"Ebony, are you okay?" he asked as he took a step towards me.

"Stay back! Stay away from me!" I yelled. I looked around to see the other men already dead. I stood up and ran to the car. Jessica got out of the car.

"Let's go." I told her.

"Where?" she asked.

"My house."

"You can't go there. They might be waiting." Logan said as he wiped his hand on his pants.

"I'm not going to listen to you."

"Well, you would have to if you want to live."

"I don't trust you."

"You don't trust me? I just killed five men to save your ass and you don't trust me. Either you're with me or without me." Logan snapped.

"Come on Ebony. Let's go with him. I don't want to die. He did save us."

'Sigh' "If we go with you, would you tell me what's going?" I asked.

"I promise, but not here." he said.

"Okay. Where can we go?"

46

"Don't worry about that right now. You will have to find out."

"Why?"

"Don't worry about it." I studied him a little. Now that I see what he is capable of, it is hard for me to trust him too. But he did save my life so I guess we are safe with him. I am still having doubts.

"Fine. How we going to get there? My car is destroyed."

"We can drive my car." Jessica said.

"Problem solved." Logan said.

"Whatever. Can we just go? Wait, before we leave, I need to go do something real quick" I said as I walked over to some bushes and heaved up this morning's breakfast.

"Okay, can leave now." I said as I turned back around after finishing, wiping my mouth.

"Sure." Jessica gave Logan her keys and we went to her Jeep. When we got in it, Logan drove off fast.

"Hey! Be careful! This Jeep is new. I just got it two months ago." Jessica said. Jessica does love this car, as if it was her baby. Logan ignored her and kept driving. Logan drove through the town, and then he turned left and drove through the woods. He stopped in front of a cave.

"We're going to stop here?" I asked.

"Yeah. Come on." He said as he got out the car.

"You got to be kidding me. I am not going to walk in there." Jessica said. I got out of the car.

"Come on Jessica." I said.

"No. I'm not going in that cave. It probably has slime and bugs or bats in there. You know how much I hate bugs. What if one crawls up my leg? I can't even think about that." she says as she shivers. Logan opened the car door and picked Jessica up and held her in his arms.

"Is that better?" He asked.

"Much better." Jessica blushed. I rolled my eyes.

"Can we just go now?!" I said, my voice a little raised.

"Don't be jealous." Logan said as he gave me his cute crooked smile. I felt my face heat up. Man, why he always do this to me. This is making me hate Logan even more because he make these feelings I have come out and he knows he's doing this.

"I' m not jealous. I just want to go just in case 'they' might be watching us."

"Yeah, okay. Follow me." He said. We walked into the cave. The more we walked into the cave, the darker it got. So Logan's eyes start to glow. This just made the situation about Logan even more mysterious. His eyes glowing did make it kind of easy to see now. The path was blocked by a wall.

"Now what are we going to do?" I asked.

"Wait." Logan said. He put Jessica down and grabbed a rock. He put it in a hole in the wall. The wall glowed and it opened to an elevator. Logan took out the rock and we got in the elevator. As soon as it closed, it went down. When it opened, it opened to this place. There were some people training and some people were on computers. Other people were eating and talking. This place was large.

"What is this place?" I asked as I looked around. That's when everything got quiet and everyone looked up at us. This woman walks up to us. She looks like she is in her early 30s. She is so pretty with her blonde hair and green eyes. She looked a little mad to see us here.

"Logan. What are you doing here?" she asked.

"He found her. I just killed five of his men at the school." When he said that, it made the woman look even angrier.

"At the school! Do you know how dangerous that was? People could have seen the whole scene."

"Sita, don't worry. I made sure no one was around. But, I did leave the bodies so the school might be in chaos right now with police." Sita closed her eyes and took a deep breath as she tried to calm down.

"You made sure no one followed you here right?" She asked.

"Yes."

"Can someone please tell me what is going on?" I interrupted, my voice a little high. Sita looked around.

"Come to my office and I will explain there." She turned to the other people.

"Get back to work people. There is nothing to see here." Sita yelled as she led us to her office. When we got there, she shut the door and sat on the other side of the desk as we sat down. Logan is still standing, leaning against the door.

"I understand you are a little confused about what is going on."

"Yes. Who the hell is the 'he' guy I keep hearing about and what do I have to do with any of this?"

"Well, first let me introduce myself. My name is Sita. I'm just going to tell you a little about history you don't know. There are two different worlds. There is the world you know, the one filled with humans. The other world, our world, is the Dark World, which is filled with witches, like me; vampires, shapeshifters, werewolves, etc."

"You're kidding right." I start laughing, but once I saw how serious Sita and Logan looked, I stopped.

"Wow. I love the Vampire Diaries and Twilight, but I did not expect to be in one." Jessica said, all excited. I rolled my eyes. Jessica is just there, but I do not know where her mind is.

"I am serious. In the Dark World, there are two sides. There is the good side, who are the Legnas, and the bad side, who are the Nomeds. We are the Legnas and the men who tried to take you are part of the Nomeds."

"So you telling me, that the 'Nomeds' you are talking about are the guys Logan just killed. How do I know you guys are not the bad guys and you are trying to kill me? What do any of this have to do with me?"

"Trust me. If we were planning on killing you, we would have killed you already. You wouldn't even hear this story right now." Logan said before Sita got to reply.

"The Nomeds' leader is Venomar. He is a very powerful original out of the Nomeds. He has one plan and one plan only- to kill you. We, the Legnas, are the ones that are protecting you."

"Why is he after me? I don't know him and I didn't even do anything to him."

"You are the last one." Sita says.

"The last what?" Logan looked over at Sita with a concerned look on his face.

"Just tell me." I said impatiently.

"You remember five years ago when your brother was killed." The familiar ache returned in my chest as I was forced to remember. Then something clicked in my head.

"Wait. How you know about my brother? My brother was killed by a wolf."

"I was there. Five years ago, I was assigned to watch over you because we heard that Venomar was going to kill you that night. In the woods, I was watching over you while you were searching for your brother. That's when I sensed Venomar. I ran to where I sensed him, but I got there too late. Venomar has already gotten to him. First he bit into him and slit his throat. I tried to stop him, but before I got to attack, he disappeared. That's when you came. The look on your face was of fear and I couldn't change out of my wolf's form. That's when I saw Venomar on the tree beside you. That's why I start walking towards you to protect you from him. That's when you ran when your brother called out to you. I was going to go after you, but I remembered your brother. When I turned around, your brother and Venomar were gone. Venomar took him." Jessica held my hand, saying "It's okay." I felt my cheeks and felt that it was wet from tears. I didn't even know I was crying. So that is what my dreams were about. Justin was talking about Venomar the whole time. So Justin's death was no accident. He was killed on purpose and I was supposed to be dead with him right now if Logan haven't protected me. But that don't explain why Venomar wanted me dead and why he still want me dead.

"Okay, I understand the part about Justin's death, but why do Venomar want me dead?"

"According to him, you are a danger to everyone. You are the last one of your kind. You hold a very powerful power." Sita said.

"What power?"

"You are the last original witch of the Barisha clan. Only you can defeat Venomar and he knows it. That is why he is trying to kill you." What Sita told me caught me by surprise that I couldn't say anything. Me? A witch?

"How am I a witch when I don't have any powers?"

"You do, you just haven't learned to use any of it."

"Okay... What is the difference between an original witch and I guess a regular witch? Why can't you just kill him yourself." I asked Sita.

"A witch can do spells and we have our powers but an original witch is even more powerful. Their spells and their powers are even more powerful. That is why one comes around every other generation. All the other original witches are dead so that is why you are the last one."

"Unfortunately, it's my fault." a familiar voice said. We all turned around.

"Laura!! We haven't seen you for years." Sita says in shock.

Chapter 9

Mom steps into the room.

"Mom? You knew about this."

"Yes sweetheart. I wanted to tell you about you and your powers, but I wanted to wait for the right time. I didn't know Venomar was still after you until Logan told me yesterday. Logan was telling me he heard you coming so we pretended to talk about something else when you came in. When I heard that Venomar was after you, I did not know that he was going to kill Justin as a threat. As soon as you told me that night what happened, I knew who was behind it, but I didn't want to scare you."

"Scare me? You kept this secret from me. All this time I thought it was my fault for Justin's death. Now I hearing this 'Venomar' guy killed Justin and want me gone too, so you guys want him destroyed. But, in order to destroy him, I have to put my life in even more danger by using powers I don't even know how to use. I can't do this."

"I'm sorry, Ebony. I didn't mean to put you in danger. If I haven't been the generation skipped, you wouldn't be the one attacked. Honey, you have people depending on you."

"I didn't even ask for them to. Don't I get a decision in any of this?" After that, I ran out of the room. This is too much to take in. My life is already messed up as it is. Now these people that I do not know are depending on me to defeat that Venomar guy to save their lives. Also finding out that mother is a part of this Legnas group and she knew all about the story behind Justin's death. This is just a lot to take in.

I ran to this door that led to a stairwell. I stopped in there and sat down on a step. I do not know what to do on this situation. Why me, out of all people. Why did such a huge burden have to be put into my hands?

"Ebony?" I turn to see Logan coming in.

"I'm here." He sits next to me on the steps.

"I'm sorry for leaving out like that. It's just this is too much for me to take in. Yesterday was just fine until today when I have to find out I'm a witch and I might possibly get killed in three days."

"I'm sorry you had to find out that way. I know how you feel. No one told me how painful it would be when transforming into a werewolf so I didn't find out until my first transformation. It was so painful, but my body finally adjusted. I was mad at parents, but I finally forgave them."

"But there is a difference. You don't have to destroy a man with powers you don't know how to use in such a short amount of time."

"Don't worry. You are stronger than you think. Sita and your mom will train you and we will not leave you alone with him. I will be by your side." I looked up into his eyes. He really meant what he said.

"Can I ask you a question? You told me you were assigned to protect me. Was flirting with me a part of the plan?" He seemed to get a little uncomfortable when I asked that. He smiled and ran his fingers through his hair.

"To tell the truth, no. That was all me. You might find it hard to believe, but I actually like you, even with your bad attitude." I turned away and felt myself blush. It was a little hard for me to believe him.

"Okay... Let's go back to the room." I got up and start walking towards the door, but Logan turned me around. I looked up into his sparkling blue eyes.

"I am telling the truth." He said as he moves a strand of my hair from my face and leans his head down. My heart starts beating real fast when our lips touched. The same strange, warm feeling came back as we kissed. He pulled back, his forehead still on mine.

"Here comes Sita." Logan says quietly. Me, still in a daze, I opened my eyes and steps back as my brain began to function again. A few seconds later, like Logan said, Sita comes in.

"Are you okay, Ebony?" Sita asked.

"Yeah. I'm okay. Sorry for leaving out like that. I had to clear my head." I took one glance at Logan, who gave me a small smile.

"I understand. Let's just go back to the room and discuss some more in there instead of in here."

"Okay." We all left out and start walking back to the room. I couldn't get my mind off the fact that Logan just told me that he likes me. I could feel myself blush, just by thinking about it. But, I have to stay in control and clear my mind if I have to defeat Venomar.

We get to the room, mom and Jessica sitting in their seats. Mom stands up and hugs me.

"I am so sorry, Ebony. I should have told you about this." she said. I feel a little embarrassed that my mom is hugging me in front of Logan.

"It's okay mom. You can let me go now."

"Oh, sorry." She says as she backs away.

"I thought about it and Logan talked with me and I decided that I will do it. I am only doing this for Justin because I feel like I still owe him. So what now? What do we have to do? We only have three days, like the little girl said, before this Venomar guy attacks."

"I thought about it and decided we can start tomorrow. Tomorrow, you will get up early and work with me and your mother on working with your powers. Then you will train later on; just in case there will have to be fighting." Sita says.

"Hey, what about me? I want to be a part of this Twilight fighting stuff." Jessica says excitedly. Sita looks over at her.

"I almost forgot that she was here. I don't know what I am going to do with you. You can't go home because you know too much. And we can't kill you. All we can do is protect you and keep you somewhere safe." she says. Jessica looks upset.

"I want to do something. Turn me into a vampire or anything." I quickly looked to Jessica like she was crazy.

"What about your family, Jessica?" I asked.

"My parents are barely home, so they won't notice any change. Also, if we make it through this, I still think it would be cool to have super strength."

"I don't know. I'll think about it. For now, you guys will be staying here with us for safety. Logan will show you to your room while I talk to Laura. We have a lot to do tomorrow. Some people will bring you food." Sita says.

"What about dad? He would find it weird that he comes home and no one is there. What if those people attack him?" I asked.

"Don't worry about him. He is out of town for a business trip. Just let Logan take both of you to your room." mom said. Jessica and I left the room with Logan and he took us to the elevator and it took us up. Once it stopped, it led us to this beautiful suite. The furniture was beautiful.

"This is all for us?" I asked, astonished.

"Yep. This is your room. I hope both of you enjoy." he says as he got back onto the elevator. Before the elevator door closed, I can see Logan giving me a smile. I can feel my face heating up as I looked away.

After the elevator door closed, I turned to Jessica and see her with a huge smile on her face.

"What was that all about? I saw that. What actually happened when Logan and you talked?" she asked.

"Nothing, I swear." I lied.

"Yeah right. I saw how both of you giving glances at each other ever since you came back. Something must have happened."

"It wasn't much. Like I said, all Logan did was talk to me... and there was a little kiss." Jessica's eyes got all wide.

"He kissed you!?! Oh my god!!" Jessica nearly screamed.

"Quiet down, Jess. It was just one kiss and you are making a big deal out of it."

"A big deal? You're the one blushing. OMG. You like him, don't you?"

"No I don't... well, a little." When I said that, she squealed. I start trying to quiet her down again.

"Let's just forget about this. Can we just change the subject, please?"

"Fine." After that, we went to check out this room. We both had our own room here and the closet was already filled with clothes. After that, we went to the living room and watched the TV. There was nothing else to do. The rest of the day was long. Like Sita said, people did bring us food. For the rest of the day, my mind was still on Venomar and this war in three days. I am so scared; I don't even know what to do. I have to learn so much in three days and I don't know what I am going to do. What if we lose and I end up dead? Even with me thinking about all these negatives, Logan's voice keep popping up in my head of what he said in the stairway.

"I will be by your side." The warm feelings are coming again.

Chapter 10

"Ebony, wake up." I didn't know who was waking me up, but it was a familiar voice.

"Mom, I'm getting up." I said as I turned over in the bed.

"Ebony?" I opened my eyes and at first all I see is blur, but my vision finally cleared up and I see it is Logan. I quickly sat up and covered myself with my covers. All I had on was some shorts and a bra.

"What the hell are you doing in here?" I hissed.

"Sorry. I tried calling, but no one answered." he says. I looked over at the clock and see its 5 o' clock in the morning.

"Why are you waking me up this early? It's 5 o'clock in the morning for Christ sake." Even though I said this, Logan wasn't paying attention. He was too busy looking at me.

"Are you naked under there?" he smiles.

"Get out!" I said through closed teeth. Logan starts backing up with his hands up.

"Fine. I just came to tell you that Sita told me to take you down to practice."

"This early... Fine. I'll be ready in 30 minutes. Now get out!" After Logan left and closed the bedroom door, I got up and went to the bathroom and took me a hot shower and brushed my teeth. After that, I left out of the bathroom, I went to the closet and got out some clothes. I put on some jeans and blue T shirt and I left my hair out. When I was finished, I left out of the room and see Logan cooking in the kitchen. I went over to see that so far he cut up some fruit and he just got finished cooking an omelet and is now working on a sauce. He looks up and smiles at me.

"Come here. Try this sauce I made for the omelet." I went over and he scooped some of the sauce on a spoon and held it to my mouth. I looked at him as I opened my mouth and took in the spoon with the sauce.

"The sauce is good." I said. All Logan did was smile. After I finished eating, we got on the elevator and it took us down. Jessica didn't go because she was still asleep.

While the elevator was going down, I can feel the tension in the elevator. I do feel a little uncomfortable since Logan almost caught me with barely any clothes on. Also I'm afraid that I might have said something in my sleep and Logan doesn't want to tell me. I turned to Logan and broke the silence.

"What happened in my room never happened. Understood?"

"What happened, exactly?"

"The "incident"... You going in my room, etc. If mom found out, she would be really mad knowing a boy almost caught her daughter half naked."

"A boy? Do you know how old I am?"

"17, I guess." he laughed when I said that.

"That is what I had to say so I can get in your school. I'm 20 years old." When he said that, I start feeling a little uncomfortable. I can't believe that this guy who is causing me to get attracted to him is 3 years older than me. And then he KISSED me! Before I got to say anything, the elevator opened to this room with shelves on each wall filled with books and there was this wooden table in the middle of the room. Before we got out of the elevator, I turned to Logan.

"Nothing happened." I hissed. All he did was shrug his shoulders. We got out of the elevator and walked over to the table. No one was in here.

"I thought you said my mom and Sita was waiting for me?"

"I never said that. I said you need to go to practice." I can feel myself starting to get angry.

"Okay... And when is this 'practice' is supposed to start?"

"6:30." I look at my watch and it is 5:50. Now I am really angry.

"So why the hell you woke me up so early? What am I supposed to do now? Just sit here for the next 40 minutes doing nothing."

"Well, we don't have to do nothing. There is one thing." he stepped closer to me as he said that. I can feel my heart beating fast.

"You wish. I prefer nothing better. Besides, you couldn't get me even if you tried." I said as I moved away quickly to the bookshelf. I can hear Logan laughing behind me.

"Oh really?" he walks over to the bookshelf and stood beside me.

"Yep." I said as I pretend to ignore him and I looked at the shelf. Even though I walked over to the bookshelf to get away from Logan, one specific book caught my attention. The name of the book is Original Witch Secrets of Tales. I took it off the shelf.

"Hey Logan, what is in this book?" I asked. He leans over to look at it.

"Why don't you look? I can't open it, or it will burn me. Only an original witch can open it." I took it off the shelf and brought it to the table. It was a little dusty so I dust it off before I opened it. Inside, the words were written in a foreign language that I did not understand. There were pictures in there, but they look like they are supposed to symbolize something and I don't know what is.

"Do you understand any of this?" Before Logan got to say anything, this picture catches my eye. It shows a drawing of a woman and a heart in the background. This picture kind of creeped me out, with a dark hooded person also in the background, the hood covering their face. What does this picture mean? Next thing I know, I hear the elevator door open and I turn to see mom and Sita getting out.

"I see you two got here early for practice." Sita says as she and mom walked over to the table with us. Her eyes widen as she looked at the book.

"No one has ever opened that book in centuries. Mother never even tried opening it. I don't even know what is in it." mom says, shocked.

"Do any of you know what this means because I don't?" Sita and mom looks at the pages and start reading. While reading, mom's face flushed away any color it had.

"Tell me what you just read." Sita turns to me with a grave look on her face.

"Well, this is basically saying that neither Venomar nor his people can kill you. That's good, but, there is a way to destroy you and so far, I believe Venomar knows it."

"What ways?" I asked, feeling myself getting scared.

"I don't think you need to know, Ebony."

"I don't care. Just tell me." I said, getting annoyed.

"You can get killed, from what the picture is showing, true love."

"What?" This just made it even more confusing.

"Only your true love, your soulmate, can kill you."

"The woman in the picture symbolizes an original witch and the hooded person symbolizes death. Love is a weak emotion so basically your soulmate holds your heart and life might take advantage of it. Let's just hope that this is just talk and nothing else. Or just hope you haven't found your soulmate." mom says. After that, everyone got quiet. I turned to Logan, who had a blank look on his face, as if he wasn't there.

"Let's just forget about this. Even if Venomar can't kill you, we still need to prepare for what he has prepared. We have two more days until the full moon." Sita says, and then looks over at Logan.

"Logan, are you okay?" she asked. At first he didn't say anything, but life was brought back to his eyes after Sita shook him a few times.

"Sorry, I was thinking about something. You can start." he gave us a smile, but something was telling me that he is keeping something from me... I mean Sita, He have nothing to explain to me.

Sita walks over to the shelf and pulled out this really thick book. It takes her to use both of her hands to haul it over to the table. When she put it on the table, it made a loud thudding sound.

"We are going through the easier spells first, then we will go over the hard ones." she says as she open the book to the first page.

"Wait... I have to go through this ENTIRE book?" I asked.

"Not all of it... Just most of it but don't worry. It should be easy for you."

"Because I am an 'original witch', right?" I rolled my eyes in annoyance.

"No, it would be easy for any beginner." Sita says as she flipped through the old yellow pages of the book, trying to find what she was looking for.

"Here it is." she says. I walk over and look in the book. The spells almost look like poems.

"The first spell you will do is making a fire. Read the spell and when you finish, point anywhere." I look down at the book and read aloud.

"Oh warmth that comes upon the hearth

Spread throughout my body

Bring fire up from palm

And make me a hot commodity." All of a sudden, I felt a weird feeling, kind of like a large energy within me, in my hands. I point my hand to the wall and out of nowhere, a fire started on it. I looked at my hand and I am in so much shock. I can't believe that I just did this. My hand is still glowing. Out of nowhere, I hear someone talking.

"Wow, it is true!" the person says. Startled, I turned around and held my hand in the direction I heard the voice. Once I saw it was Jessica, it was too late.

Chapter 11

The fire start going towards Jessica, but thank god she jumped out of the way. So instead of it hitting her, it hit the bookshelf, causing the books to catch on fire. Before a big damage was able to happen, mom and Sita held their hands towards it and water start hitting the books, the fire died down completely.

"I am so sorry." I said to mom and Sita. I can hear Logan chuckling, causing me to feel even more embarrassed.

"It's okay. All we need to do is work on you controlling your powers."

"I'm so sorry Ebony. I didn't mean to startle you." Jessica said, looking a little embarrassed, just like how I was feeling.

"It's okay Jessica." I said as I looked over at Logan, who I can tell is trying to keep himself from laughing some more, causing me to feel a little more embarrassed about the situation. I can feel my cheeks warming up, probably turning my cheeks red. Mom looks at me and then at Logan and frowned. Oh no. I know that look and I don't like it.

"Well, let us all forget what had happened. Jessica, how did you get here?" Sita asked. Jessica blushes before she says anything. Oh my gosh! I definitely know that look. That is her 'I'm in love' look. Next thing I know, this cute guy with blonde hair and green eyes walks from the elevator. He had smooth pale skin and he was tall.

"I'm sorry, Sita. She was in the elevator when I got on and she was asking where you were." he has a nice Irish accent too. I leaned over to Logan.

"What is he?" I whispered.

"He's a vampire. He's not an original, but he has the power of pain illusion. Josh projects the illusion of being in extremely intense physical pain into others minds, incapacitating them." he whispers back.

"It's good that you brought her here." Sita says. Josh nods and looks at Jessica and smiles.

"I'm leaving now. We shall meet again." he says as he grabbed her hand and kissed it. Jessica blushed some more.

"I hope so." she says as Josh got back on the elevator. Jessica almost followed him, but I stopped her.

"Jessica!" I called for her. She looked at me and then at the closed elevator door. She pouts and walks back towards me.

"Jessica, what was that?" I asked, but she didn't seem to be listening. She ignored my question.

"Ebony, I think I'm in love."

"I thought you was 'in love' with Adam." Jessica still looked a little dazed.

"Adam? Oh yeah. I'm over him now. Did you see Josh? He kissed my hand. What a gentleman. Also, he's a vampire, which makes him even hotter." she says. I rolled my eyes.

"Whatever."

"Sorry to interrupt, but Ebony, we have to teach you as much as we can to prepare you." Sita says.

"I'm sorry. We can continue." I said as I walked back over to the table.

"Now you need to learn to protect yourself from any creature. Logan?" Sita looked at him and nodded her head. He looked at me and gave me a small smile. Next thing I know, he began to transform into a wolf. A BIG wolf. He still looks the same, even after 5 years. He still has his dark gray and white fur and blue eyes. I can see a smile on his face as he howled. He looked at me and growled. Next thing I know, he start running towards me. Just in time, I moved out of the way before he starts transforming back to human form.

"That wasn't the kind of protecting I was talking about, but you did well." Sita says. I'm still in shock from what have just happened.

"What the hell! You are willing to kill me to see if I am able to defend myself."

"I wouldn't put it that way. I wasn't expecting for you to duck out of the way. Witches have the power of the mind. We can bring our victim extreme migrating headaches, but yours should be even more powerful."

"So, how am I supposed to do this?"

"Just treat it like an instinct. All you have to do is concentrate." mom says. She looks over to Logan.

"Are you ready?" she asked him. He nodded and walked over to the other side of the room. I was expecting him to transform again, but instead, he stuck out his claws and start running towards me, his eyes glowing. I stuck my hands up towards him, but he didn't stop.

"Why is it not working?" I yelled behind me.

"You have to concentrate." mom says. I turned back to Logan and I am looking Logan straight in his eyes. He is standing right in front of me, a smile on his face. His eyes are still glowing, which is kind of creeping me out.

"You can't do it. It's okay if you're a little weak right now." he says quiet enough for only me to hear.

"I'm not weak..." All of a sudden, I feel a huge energy building up in me. I know what this is. I looked into his eyes and concentrated. Next thing I know, Logan start groaning and he end up on his knees, holding his head. I bend down so I am looking him right into his blue eyes.

"Now you are the weak one." I gave him a smile.

"I will get you back." Before he got to finish, he grabbed his forehead again and start groaning again. I got up and walked back to mom, Sita and Jessica.

"Good job, Ebony." You accomplished your task."

"Thanks. I couldn't do it without a little motivation from Logan." I turned to him and smiled. Logan, already back on his feet, gave me a fake smile. After that, for 6 more hours, we practiced more spells. It was kind of fun because for some of them, Logan was like our lab rat and I know he didn't enjoy it.

"I have to go now. We are done for today. You have your own copy of this spell book in your room. So whenever you get the chance, you study. Your mother and I have to go to a meeting, so you can do whatever you want but don't do anything crazy." Sita says as both her and mom got on the elevator. As soon as the door closed, I knew what I was up to now.

Chapter 12

"So, what are we going to do now?" I asked as we just stood here in the room.

"Well, lunch should be ready. Everyone should be in the dining hall." Jessica head shot up as soon as she heard that, she got all excited, but cooled down.

"I'm not hungry..." I start to say, but Jessica nudged me hard in my side with her elbow.

"Oww! I guess I'm a little hungry." I said as I rubbed my side.

"Okay, I'll take you there then." Jessica smiled as we got on the elevator with him. It starts going down.

"Just to let you guys know, I suggest you go find food in the witch or werewolf section. In the vampire section, all they have is blood or raw meat." After he said that, the elevator door opened to this huge room filled with people, whatever creature they are. The way the dining hall was designed was a mixture of a cafeteria, by how the tables were, and a buffet. When we got off the elevator, everyone got quiet and looked in our direction. I start feeling a little nervous.

"Umm, Logan..." I start to say something, but when I turned around, only Jessica was standing there. Logan was gone.

"Where did he go?" I asked, but all Jessica did was shrug her shoulders. Soon, the people went back to doing what they were doing. That is when I start to relax.

"Come on, Ebony. Let's go get something to eat. I'm starving."

"No you're not. You're only here so you can drool over that Josh guy." Jessica gave me a shocked look.

"That is not true. I didn't eat breakfast. Can a girl just eat?"

"Okay." I said sarcastically. We walked over to the food. I got me a chicken salad with French dressing while Jessica got french fries. We walked over to the drink section.

"What is this? It looks good." She goes over to a dark red drink. By first glance, I can already tell what it is.

"Um Jessica? You know what, never mind." I know a good friend like me is supposed to stop her from getting blood, but I just want a good laugh after all this chaos that is going on in my life right now. Before Jessica got the chance to pull down the lever to pour the blood in her cup, all I know, I see a swift breeze and out of nowhere, Josh is standing beside Jessica. He put his hand on top of hers to stop her from pouring it.

"You do not want any of that, trust me." he said.

"Why?" she says, a little surprised to see him there.

"That is human blood. Unless you are a vampire or you are just a strange girl, I suggest you don't drink that." Jessica face turned so red. I bet she feel so embarrassed right now with her new 'love'.

"Thanks, I didn't know. Thank you for saving me." she said as she twirled her hair playfully, smiling at him. Josh, his hand still on hers, pulled down the lever and the blood poured into the cup.

"Wait. What are you doing? I thought you said I shouldn't drink that." he smiled at her as he grabbed the cup from her hand.

"I know, but I can." he put the cup to his lips and drank some. His eyes are closed, but when he stopped drinking, he opened his eyes and they went from pitch black back to his green eyes.

"Delicious." he said as he smiled down at her. All it did was made her blush but she blushed even more every time he said something to her.

71

"So, how did you girls get down here?" he asked.

"Well, Logan brought us down here, but then he ditched us." I said.

"Oh, Logan is sitting over at my table. Do you want to sit with us?"

"Well,..." I start to deny the offer, but Jessica quickly interrupted me.

"Oh course we do." Jessica said all cheerfully. A little too excited. Josh laughed from the response.

"Okay, follow me." he start walking as we followed him.

"What the hell was that? You don't want me to be happy. You saw how sexy he looked when he drank that."

"What are you talking about? You just met the guy and you are already drooling over him." I whispered back.

"No I'm not."

"Fine. Whatever." I am not going to argue with her. We get to the table and Logan is already sitting down with a cheeseburger, chili cheese fries, and a coke. Since it was a booth, there were two sides. Josh sat on the other side and Jessica quickly sat next to him. That mean I was stuck sitting next to Logan and he knew I didn't want that. He looked up at me and smiled. I sighed, put my tray down, and sat down next to him.

"Why did you leave us? We had to find our way around. Thanks to Josh, we wouldn't have found you." I said to him.

"Calm down. I said I will take you to the diving hall, that's it. You didn't have much trouble finding the food. You got what you want."

"I found them at the blood section. Jessica was about to get some."

"You should have let her do it, even though she probably wouldn't have drank it any way." Logan said.

"I know, even though that would have been kind of sexy." Jessica perked up at that.

"Really?" she asked. Oh no, I know what she is thinking right now.

"Yeah. I love a girl who is daring." Josh said as he smiled at her. Jessica calmed down and gave him a flirtatious smile back. I rolled my eyes as I start to eat my salad.

"What a coincidence. I am daring." she said as she grabbed Josh's cup of blood and drank it down. I dropped my fork, shocked that Jessica is really doing this. I looked over and Logan is shocked and so is Josh. When she finished, she put the cup down. There was a little trickle of blood on her lip, but she wiped it with a napkin. She looked so normal, but she then start looking like she needed to throw up, but all she did was burp.

"Excuse me." she said as she covered her mouth.

"Wow. You don't feel sick at all?" I asked.

"No. It was a little weird, but that's it." she said. Josh smiled and whispered in her ear. Her face turned a little red.

"Right now?" she asked all excited. He nodded his head.

"Excuse us." They both said as they both got up and quickly walked away. I already know what they are going to do, but I can't believe Jessica just left me with Logan.

"So, at least she got what she wanted." he said.

"Yep."

"So..."

"So what?"

"What do you want?" I almost choked on a piece of salad.

"Excuse me?" he smiled at me.

"Well, I don't know if you ever noticed, but you are kind of dull. What do you want to do?"

"Oh, That's what you meant." he looked confused, but then he finally got it.

"Oh, I already know you want me. I don't need to question that."

"Ha! You are so funny. In your dreams."

"You may not think this now, but watch." We finished eating our food and got up.

"I want to show you something." he said as we dumped our tray.

"What is it?"

"It's a surprise." he said as we walked to the elevator. We got in the elevator and he hit a button. There are just so many buttons in here.

"How do you know which button to click, even if they don't have names on them?

"It took a lot of memorizing." he said as the elevator start going up. When it stopped, it opened to this forest.

"What is it?" I asked as I walked in.

"This is my room."

"Why is it like the forest? Why don't you have a regular room?"

"This is something I feel comfortable in, especially when I am in my wolf form. Follow me." We start walking through the forest and I can hear rushing water.

"Is that what I think it is?" I asked.

"Yep."

"You have a water fall in your room?" we walked from behind the trees and I see it. It was an actual waterfall. It was so beautiful.

"Come on." he said as we walked to the side of it and started climbing. I climbed behind him. When we made it to the top, I can now see everything. We sat down on one of the edge and stuck our feet in the rushing water.

"I used to live in Minnesota and my parents and I used to live in a cabin in the forest so we can live near our hunting ground. My father was the head of the pack so he was barely home because he was too busy with the men. My mom was the only one there for me and she took care of me. The times my father came home was cool. He would start training me and teaching me how to fight, trying to get me ready for my first transformation, and I was only 6 years old. My first transformation was when I was 10. That was the first time my father seemed to be proud of me. One day, my father took me and the rest of the pack hunting and that was my first time. I have to admit, it was kind of fun hanging out with my dad. After a few hours of chasing deer, catching them, we went home." Then he stopped. I can tell something happened. I knew that there was more to it. But I am not going to force it out of him. Even though he was looking down, I can see the sadness in his eyes.

"Let's do what I brought you here for." he said as he smiled and stood up. He took off his shirt, now showing his bare skin, but he kept on his shorts.

"And what are we doing, exactly?" I hope it is not what I think he is talking about.

"This." he said as he took off his shoes and socks and jumped from the edge of the waterfall into the water. For a second, I thought he wasn't coming up, but then he came up. I was a little relieved he wasn't talking about sex, but this was crazier.

"Come on." he yelled up at me as he moved his hair out of his face.

"Are you crazy? I am not jumping in there."

"Do you know how to swim?"

"Yes."

"Then what is the problem?"

"I am not jumping off any cliff."

"Why are you so dull? Don't you do anything fun or daring?"

"Yes. I did daring things before."

"Like what?"

"I rode a roller coaster. Jessica basically had to drag me on it, knowing my fear for them."

"You're kidding, right? I see why you don't have a boyfriend." I know he didn't just go there.

"What is that supposed to mean. I can get a boyfriend if I want. I just chose not to get one. But you know what, I'll do it." I took off my shirt and pants, leaving me only with my bra and underwear. I looked down at the water. I didn't notice how far up I was until now, causing me to get a little nervous.

"Come on, Ebony. You can do this." I thought to myself as I jumped. As soon as I landed in the water, I almost panicked, but then I realized I was alive so I swam up. When I reached the surface, I didn't see Logan anywhere.

"Logan?" I looked around, but I didn't see him. I know he didn't just ditch me again. Next thing I know, I feel someone touch my side. I quickly turned around and see Logan standing there.

"What the hell Logan. You almost gave me a heart attack."

"Sorry. But wasn't that fun?"

"Which part? The one almost gave me a heart attack or the jump?"

"Haha, very funny. I'm talking about the jump."

"It was okay." I said as I pushed my hair out of my face.

"Just okay?"

"Yeah. It was just a jump."

"Yeah. Okay." He said sarcastically as he starts getting closer to me.

"What are you doing?" I asked as I backed up.

"You remember at the practice? I told you I would get you back."

"No. don't you dare." I said as I backed up some more, laughing.

"Watch me." he said as he smiled.

"Well, before you do anything, my mom is here." he looked behind him. I looked over at the waterfall. I ducked back in the water and swam towards it. I knew I got to it as soon as I felt little pounding in the water. When I got back up, I was in front of the waterfall. I turned around and Logan is standing right there. I almost screamed when I saw him.

"Are you still trying to get a heart attack again?" I said as I put my hand on my chest, trying to slow down my heart beat. He starts laughing.

"That is not funny."

"Really? I thought it was hilarious." he said as he stopped laughing, but still smiling.

"Well, no it wasn't." he start moving closer to me.

"You know you look so cute when you're mad." he said as he is right in front of me. I tried backing away, but I was already against the rocky wall of the waterfall. He brushed a strand of my hair out of my face. I can feel my heart beat fast.

"We can't Logan."

"We can't what?"

"We can't do this."

"Why? I want it to happen and I can tell you do too because your heart is beating fast." I was about to ask him how he know, but then I remembered he is a werewolf.

"I know, but that doesn't matter. This is wrong. You are 3 years older than me."

"I don't care. It's what you feel that matters." he steps closer, leaving, no space between us. My heart is beating faster.

"Now the question is, do you have feelings for me?" he asked.

"I-I don't know. I have to go." I tried to walk away, but Logan wouldn't move. I looked him in the eyes and the urge in me to kiss him wouldn't go away, so I did what surprised me. I kissed him and he kissed me back. The same strange feelings start coming back. He backed away, causing me to feel a little disappointed. He can tell, but he smiled.

"Let's go." he said.

Chapter 13

After we grabbed our clothes, he let me wear his shirt, which was long enough to be a short dress. We walked back over to the elevator and when we got on, he clicked a button.

"Where are we going now?"

"Back to your room."

"Oh." I said a little disappointed. I guess he really took me serious when I said I have to go. The elevator opened and we walked into the suite. I looked in Jessica's room and I see she is not in there.

"Well, I guess I will you see you later or tomorrow." he said as he start walking toward the elevator.

"Wait, you leaving me now, all alone?" he turned back to me and smiled.

"At least don't leave your shirt." I said as I smiled back.

"Of course I wouldn't leave you." he said as he walked up to me and kissed me. I kissed him back as I wrapped my arms around his neck. We walked back to my room and ended up falling on my bed. I couldn't help laughing and he laughed too. He stopped and looked at me and smiled.

"You are so beautiful." he said. I giggled and we kissed again. Things start getting heated and a part of me was thinking "What am I doing?" I shouldn't be here with him or like this with him, but there is something, this desire, that is running through me. He is a pain in the ass, but an attractive pain in the ass.

"Ebony?" I opened my eyes to see mom standing there in my doorway.

"Mom?!" I quickly pushed Logan away and sat up.

"What in the world is going on?"

"Mom, it's not what you think..." I looked down and see I still have on Logan's shirt and all Logan has on is his pants.

"Well, it may look like what you think, but I swear nothing happened." I said to her.

"What is going on?" Next person who comes in is Sita. This is so humiliating, I feel like dying from humiliation. I look over at Logan, who was sitting up too, and see he is a little embarrassed too.

"Logan, what have you done? I am so sorry about this, Laura."

"We need to talk, Ebony." mom said sternly. I turned to Logan.

"I'm so sorry for this. Can we talk later?" I said low enough for only him to hear.

"No, I'm sorry. I'll see you later." he touched my hand softly before he left out. Sita followed him and both of them got on the elevator. Mom sighed and sat next to me on the bed.

"I'm sorry I yelled at you like that, but we need to talk."

"What is it, mom?"

"You and I need to talk and I think now is the time. What is going on between you and Logan need to stop, and I mean now." what she just said hit me like a ton of bricks.

"What are we doing now?"

"This fling that is going on between the two of you. You think I don't notice, but I do."

"Mom, there is no fling going on between the two of us. Besides, it's none of your business what is going on between us." mom looked taken back from what I have said.

"I'm sorry mom. I didn't mean it like that." I said.

"I know. It's just I don't want you to get distracted. You have a lot of practice to do. I'm just trying to keep you safe."

"Mom, I can take care of myself. And why would I need protection from Logan? All Logan did was help me."

"And you sure all he did was help you? Or is there something else going on between the two of you?"

"Mom, we kissed, that's it." A part of me knew I was lying. Mom looked at me for a while, as if I was lying.

"Fine. I have to go. I just came up here to check up on you, but I see you are fine. But don't forget what I said. You have to concentrate on this. Venomar is a stubborn guy, and he will not give up so easily. You will have to destroy him." she said as we walked to the elevator.

"Mom, I can do this."

"I know you can." she said as she hugged me.

"Oh, and make sure you give Logan back his shirt." I looked down and I feel my face heating up. She smiled and got on the elevator.

"Wait... mom? Does dad know about us? About our powers I mean." Mom starts looking sad.

"Unfortunately, no. I never told him. That is why I haven't been here in a long time. I had to choose to either keep the both of you safe and leave or stay and put the ones I love in danger. But it look like I didn't accomplish that." she said as the elevator door closed. I went to the living room and turned on the TV, even though I wasn't paying attention. All I was thinking about was what mom said. I know I should be listening to her and staying focused without distractions, such as Logan. But I can't because a part of me knows that no matter what, there will always be a connection between us and the feelings I'm feeling will never go away, no matter how hard I try to get over it.

Chapter 14

After an hour of watching TV, I hear the elevator door open. I looked behind me and see Jessica and Josh getting off. Jessica looks over at my direction.

"Ebony? I almost didn't see you." she said all excited.

"I have to go." Josh said.

"Right now?" she said, looking all sad.

"I will see you tomorrow."

"Okay."

"Bye my love." he said as he pulled her in and they kissed. I feel like I have to puke, just looking at these love birds.

"Bye, Ebony." he said as he got back on the elevator. When it closed, Jessica ran over to me and jumped on the couch, all excited.

"Ebony, I think I'm in love."

"You said that before with Adam."

"This is different. He is different... and hot." I looked into her eyes and she is telling the truth. I never seen her this happy before.

"So, what happened after you and Josh ditched me."

"We did not ditch you. We left you with Logan."

"Exactly my point. Tell me what happened after you two left."

"Well, after we left, he took me to his suite and let's just say things got steamy, but we didn't do it or anything. Then we cuddled and talked and he showed me his little sister. She is the little girl who came to you yesterday. Her name is Isabella and she is 6 years old. Her power is that she can tell the future. She wanted to come see you, but we didn't know you were going to be in here. So yeah, I had a great time." she sighed as she daydreamed.

"Earth to Jessica." I said as I laughed.

"I'm sorry. I'm just so happy. So, how were things between you and Logan? I know the both of you..." she stopped as she looked at what I was wearing. She just noticed that I was wearing Logan's shirt.

"No you didn't. Isn't that the shirt Logan was wearing earlier?" she said, all smiling.

"It's not what you think. We didn't do it." I said as I laughed.

"Then what are you doing with his shirt on?"

"It's a long story."

"Tell me now."

"Fine." I told Jessica everything that has happened and the same time I was reliving the moments, which brought great feelings within me.

"That is so romantic, but your mom really walked in on you two?"

"Yep. After Logan and Sita left, mom gave me a big lecture on how I need to concentrate only on beating Venomar. Maybe she is right."

"No, you can't give up on Logan. You guys were meant to be together."

"I am just so confused with all these mixed feelings. I don't know what to do. I just need some time to think. I will be right back."

"Do you want me to go with you?"

"No. I will be right back. I just need to change."

"Okay." she said. I went to my room and took off Logan's shirt and my remaining clothes to take a shower. When I was finished, I put on a gray low scoop tee shirt and jeans. After I finished getting dressed, I left out and got on the elevator. Jessica was too busy on the phone talking to Josh, laughing and flirting with him. When the elevator door closed, I just clicked any button. I don't care where I go; I just want to get out of here. The elevator starts going up. It took a while until it stopped. When the door opened, it led to outside, but this was not the cave. It was like I was in another dimension. People are walking past me, but they don't look like regular people. There were different animals walking around and the streets. Kids are actually out tonight, playing in the streets, but not the usual playing. Some of the kids start chasing each other and they were turning into panthers, wolves, foxes, bears, tigers, etc. There are some kids who are vampires, with their super speed, and kids who are witches, using their powers on the other kids and some objects. That is when I knew where I was... I was in the Dark World.

Chapter 15

"So, there is another world." I thought to myself. I walked down the street and people were looking at me. It was like a small town, with the stores and buildings to the side. The only difference between this world and the world I am used to is that this one seems a little gloomy. The people were all different.

As I was walking, I came upon a club. The music was blasting through the doors. I walked up to the door, but the bouncer stopped me from entering. This guy was huge, so I'm guessing he is a shapeshifter.

"Do you belong here?" he asked.

"What is this place?"

"Look, if you want to come in, you will have to pay." he said impatiently. I almost tried to get my wallet from my pocket, but then I remembered I left my wallet in my room.

"She's with me." I hear a guy say from behind me. His voice is not familiar, so he's not Logan. The guy walked in front of me and handed the bouncer money. The bouncer nodded and stepped aside as we walked in.

"Um, thank you for paying for me."

"No problem." he said as we sat down at the bar. He looked handsome with his short, blonde hair and blue eyes. His pale skin shows me that he must be a vampire. He look no older than his mid-20s.

"What is this place?"

"This is club Underworld. This is where we go and have wild parties. You have to be careful, though. There are some people who you can't trust and some you just have to stay away from." he said as he gave me a big smile. There was something dangerous about him that I just couldn't put my finger on.

"Which one are you?"

"You tell me."

"I don't know. I don't even know I should be talking to you."

"You can trust me, Ebony. I did help you get in here."

"That is true... Wait, I never told you my name."

"Yes you did."

"No I didn't. Who are you?"

"I am a hybrid, half vampire and half wolf. We finally meet again, face to face. I have been waiting for this day to come. I remember you, but you don't remember me."

"Umm, you still haven't told me who you are." now this guy is creeping me out.

"I am Venomar, nice to meet you." Once he said that, I quickly moved over. All he did was smile.

"Get away from me!"

"Come on, we are just acquaintances who are getting to know each other. So, how is life after your brother? I remember you as a little girl. I wanted that night to be the first time we meet, but that stupid wolf boy stopped that from happening. I have been watching you for years, making sure you were okay until this day finally comes. I tried to make it yesterday, but that same stupid wolf boy stopped it from happening again. I was actually thinking about killing him, but what fun would that be?"

"What do you want from me? Why can't you just leave me alone?"

"I want you dead. But, so far things are not going as planned. Now, I would kill you right now, but..."

"But you can't, can you? You already know you can't."

"I know I can't. The one that holds your heart can kill you. I have been doing my readings."

"Look, you are wasting your time and mines with all of this. I would have a normal life if it wasn't for you. My brother would still be here if it wasn't for you. You messed up everything for something you can't even take from me."

"All I can say is wait. Enjoy the time you have right now. When I set a goal, I make sure it is done unless I die trying."

"I guess death it is for you." I said.

"Ebony, move away from him." the guy who said that pulled me up from the seat and moved me behind him. That is when I saw it was Logan.

"You again. Do I have to kill you just to keep you away? Everywhere she is, you are there with her." Venomar said, all serious now.

"Don't you dare touch Logan. He did nothing to you." I snapped at him. That is when Venomar looked from me to Logan.

"This is wonderful. The two lovebirds. I will definitely see you later. The next time I do see you, you will definitely be dead afterwards." he said as he walked away. Logan turned to me with a worried look on his face.

"Are you okay? Did he touch you or did anything to you?"

"He did nothing to me. Can we just get out of here... please?"

"Okay, come on." he said as he takes me outside.

"How did you find me?"

"I saw you enter into the club with Venomar. What are you doing out here? I thought you were supposed to be in your room."

"I am so sorry. I didn't know that the guy was Venomar. I just wanted to go anywhere but staying in the room. The elevator led me here."

"It's okay. Let me just take you back to your room. I have to tell Sita about this, but you don't have to worry about any of this." We start walking back to where I got off the elevator, but the elevator wasn't there.

"What happened to the elevator? It was right here."

"Follow me. It does this so that not just anyone can get on." We walk to an abandoned building and walked in. It was dark in here, but the moonlight shone in the window, making it easier for me to make my way through. We walked up the flights of stairs until we got to the roof top. Logan wiped off the door and then opened it. On the other side of the door was the elevator, so we got on and he pushed a button as the door shut.

"How did you do that?"

"The door is like a scanner. It recognizes my handprint. It should do that for you too." We stayed quiet as the elevator start going down.

"Do you know what he was talking about?" I asked.

"Don't worry about him. All you have to do is practice more on your magic and you should be good. Just get enough sleep tonight and you should be okay." When he finished saying this, the elevator opened back to my suite. Jessica was still in her place on the couch, but I can smell food cooking. We walked out of the elevator and I looked over to the kitchen and I see Josh cooking. Josh looked up at us and smiled.

"Hey. Jessica invited us here. I hope that's alright?"

"Us?" I asked, but then Isabella came running in from the back to me and jumped up. I caught her and picked her up.

"Ebony!!!" she said all excited as she smiled at me.

"Hey Isabella. It's nice actually seeing a smile on your face this time." I said as I put her back down.

"She kept calling your name and saying how she wanted to see you, so I brought her here." Josh said as he put a pan in the oven.

"It's okay. I could use some company. What are you making?"

"Pizza."

"You have the ingredients to make a pizza?" Logan asked.

"No. This was frozen in a box in the freezer."

"It doesn't matter. Josh is a great cook." Jessica said as she walked over to Josh. I rolled my eyes as I tried not to laugh. I look over to Logan and he is just shaking his head. I looked down at Isabella and she just looks confused.

"What?" Jessica asked, her face turning red.

"Nothing, just everyone sit down in the living room. We need to talk." Logan said. We walked over and sat down. Logan sat next to me on the couch while Jessica sat in one of the chairs and Josh stood next to her.

"What's wrong?" Josh asked.

"As you know, we have one more day to prepare for what happens. While we were out, Ebony ran into Venomar. Nothing happened..."

"Are you okay, Ebony?" Jessica asked, looking all concerned.

"Yes, Jess. I'm fine." I said.

"Back to what I was saying, I talked with the pack earlier today about this situation. We have been waiting for this day to come so we are training. What about your group, Josh?"

"We have been doing the same thing too. The new born vampires that came recently are being trained for this. Now the question is, what is Venomar planning on doing? Do we have enough people to beat him?"

"I don't know, but there is no doubt that he will bring his army."

"Wait... the war is going to be here? How will we know it has started?" I asked.

"We will know. Venomar never try to hide anything."

"I wish I could go with you guys." Jessica says.

"What are you going to do? You can't do anything but get hurt. I don't want to risk your safety." Josh says, all serious.

"I know that I won't be helpful like this. That is why I want you to change me." That is when it got quiet in here.

"I need to go check on the pizza." Josh said as he quickly walked over to the oven and opened it.

"I don't think that is a good idea, Jessica." Logan said.

"I agree." Josh said from in the kitchen.

"But, it's what I want. I want to help out my best friend and myself. I never thought that I would do something extraordinary in life until now. Now I know what I want."

"Jess, what about your parents?" I asked.

"What parents? They don't care about what I do or where I go. Come on Josh. Let me be your Bella." Jessica said as she walked over to him. I'm shocked that she just went Twilight in this situation. Jess need to slow down on all the supernatural stuff.

"Jessica, I can't. You don't know how painful it is during transformation. I don't want to be the cause of your pain."

"As long as you are with me, I'm good. I want to stay with you."

"Is this a romance movie now?" Logan mumbled irritably.

"Shut up." I said as I hit him in the arm.

"What!?!" he said as he rubbed his arm. I just ignored him and focused my attention back to Josh and Jessica.

"Are you sure?" Josh asked.

"Yes." Josh turned to Logan.

"Is it okay?"

"I really don't care. It's your choice, man." Logan said irritably.

"Let's do it then." Josh said as he smiled down at Jessica.

Chapter 16

"Are you serious?" Jessica said, all excited.

"If you want it, I will do it to make you happy."

"Thank you!!!" She screamed as she jumped up on him and kissed him.

"Get a room." Logan said.

"Shut up." Jessica said as she shot a glance at Logan. Jessica turned to Josh.

"I want to start the transformation now."

"Right now?"

"Yeah. The fight is in two days. Remember, I still need to train."

"Fine."

"What about the pizza?" Logan asked.

"Yeah." Isabella said,

"It's done. You can eat." Josh said. So, while Isabella, Logan, and I sat down at the table and start eating the pizza, Josh started his transformation on Jessica. Both of them were sitting on the couch, facing each other, and Josh was holding her hands.

"This might hurt." Josh told Jessica.

"What you..." Before Jessica could finish her question, Josh bit her on the wrist. She used her other hand to cover her mouth to keep herself from screaming, but I can still see the pain in her eyes, but then her face became calm.

"That looks painful." I said.

"It is." Logan and Isabella said at the same time. I looked at both of them, then back at Jessica. She was leaning against the couch and she was getting paler. I got up quickly, but Logan stopped me.

"Let me go. He is taking too much." I said.

"I know." Logan said. I looked at him and frowned.

"You're not going to stop him?"

"No."

"Why the hell not?"

"Because, if I do, she would die."

"Hello? It already looks like she is dying."

"Just watch, Ebony." 'sigh' I looked back to where Jessica is. I'm starting to get worried. When Josh was finished, he bit into his wrist, ripping skin. Blood start pouring as he put his wrist to her mouth. Even though she was so weak, she grabbed Josh hand and drank greedily on Josh's blood. Josh held her as she drank. She drank until she fell asleep. She was still too pale.

"Are you done now?" I asked Josh.

"Not yet. I need to do one last thing." Josh said. I frowned.

"What is the 'last thing?"

"This. I'm sorry, Jessica." Next thing I know, he twist Jessica's neck. I can hear the crack.

"What the... you just killed her!" I tried to run to him, but Logan stopped me. All I feel is rage.

"I know." Josh laid Jessica down on the couch.

"You look satisfied with this! I thought you love her."

"I do."

"Then why did you kill her? How is she supposed to get through the transformation and she is dead."

"This is the transformation! You don't watch any TV, do you? You know, some of the things they say about us vampires are true."

Now I was confused.

"What?" Josh sighed.

"In order for her to go through the transformation, as soon as I feed her my blood, she would have to die." He said. I blush with embarrassment.

"Oh."

"Yeah... Oh."

"Then when is she supposed to wake up?"

"Tomorrow. Then she can start feeding. Also, I would help her with her training for the fight."

"Will her neck heal?"

"Yeah. Since she is going through the transformation, her neck should be healing right now."

"You almost scared me half to death."

"I can tell."

"Hey. How would you feel if your best friend just got her neck twisted off?"

"She does have a point." Logan said.

"Yep." Isabella said as she took another slice of pizza.

"You could have warned me." I said.

"I know. I know. I'm sorry."

'Sigh' "It's alright." Before I could say anything else, the elevator door opened and mom came out. We all froze when mom saw Jessica. She looked at us, then back at Jess.

"Hey mom." I said.

"Ebony... what is going on?" she asked.

"I don't know what you mean."

"What are you guys doing?"

"Just hanging out... Right guys?"

"Yeah." Josh and Logan said at the same time. Mom looked away from me, then back at Jessica. She ran to Jessica.

"Why is Jessica so pale?" I see mom put her hand on her. Her hand glowed. After a couple of minutes, she took her hand away from Jessica so quickly. She stood up and looked at Josh.

"You turned her?" Josh, Logan and I looked at each other, then at mom.

"Surprise." we said.

"There is no surprise. I came up here because I got a call from her mom, Mrs. Austin, saying that she wants to talk to Jess."

"Well tell her that Jess is asleep and she can't talk right now." I said.

"She is sleeping." Isabella said as she played with the cheese on her pizza. Mom rubbed her temples with her fingers as she sighed.

"Fine. I will tell her, but before I go, I have a question. Why did you change Jessica, Josh? Did she hurt herself badly because she can be clumsy. She always been clumsy ever since she was a little girl. Or..."

"She wanted me to change her, Mrs. Jenkins. I'm sorry if you don't agree with the decision I made." Mom looked down at Jessica.

"When does she wake up?"

"She should be awake tomorrow."

"Well, you can't leave her here with Ebony, just in case she wakes up early."

"I know. I'm taking her with me to my room for the night."

"Do Sita know about this transformation?"

"Not yet. I will tell her when I see her." Mom looked at Josh for a while, as if she was trying to read his mind.

"Fine. I'm leaving now." she said as she got on the elevator. When the door closed, Josh start to pick up Jessica.

"We should be going too. It is Isabella's bedtime so I will see you guys tomorrow. Give me good luck when I tell Sita about this.' Josh said as he held Jessica in his arms, her arms and legs dangling.

"I want to stay with Ebony... please." Isabella whined.

"You will see her tomorrow, Izzy. Come on."

"Please." She said, giving Josh the puppy face with her big blue eyes.

"Okay... But who will I get to share my banana split with in the room."

"Never mind. Bye Ebony. I want ice cream." She said as she ran after Josh in the elevator. We all laughed as the door closed. I went into the kitchen and put the remaining pizza into the fridge and Logan put the pan in the dish washer. So far we have not said one word to each other. When we were finished, Logan start walking to the elevator.

"I guess I should leave too." he said.

"Wait, you are leaving me too?"

"If you want me to stay, I can stay."

"Please stay. I don't want to be alone right now."

"Okay. What do you want to do?"

"Help me with the spells. I have to get this right... so I am going to read the whole book." When I said that, Logan looked at me like I was crazy.

"All of it tonight?"

"At least try. Come on. How hard can it be?" After that, we walked back into the living room and I went to the bookshelf and grabbed the spell book. I sat next to Logan and we went over every spell. At least most of it. Before I got to finish it, we fell asleep.

Chapter 17

As I was waking up, I almost stretched, but I was touching something warm and hard. I looked around and noticed that I was still in the living room. I paid more attention to my surroundings and noticed that I was lying on top of Logan, me hugging him, my head on his chest and his arm around me. Even though I found this a little awkward, I had to admit that I was comfortable. It was almost as if I belonged there in his arms, even though I will never tell him that. I looked up at his face and he was still asleep. He looked so relaxed. That is when the same strange feelings I feel when I'm with Logan came back. Some of his hair was hanging in his face and I brushed it out of the way. I looked at my watch to see what time it is and I see it is 11:30 in the morning.

"Oh crap, we are late for practice." I said as I pushed Logan's arm from around me. That caused him to wake up. I got up and start to run to my room.

"What's wrong, Ebony?" he said as he got up and rubbed his eyes.

"Sita and mom are going to kill us. We are late for training." I yelled out to him from in my room. I hurried and took a quick shower and brushed my teeth. After that, I went the dresser and grabbed some jeans and a tank top and my undergarments and put them on. I didn't bother doing anything to my hair, so I'm letting it air dry. When I left out of my room, I didn't see Logan anywhere, but I did see a note on the table. I went over to it and read the notes. Logan was telling me that he went to his room to clean up and change and for me to meet him in the training room. Since I wasn't hungry, I just went to the elevator. Thank goodness Logan wrote down on the note which button to click to get to the training room or I would have got lost just like last night.

I got on the elevator and clicked the button that led me to the floor. Before the door opened, there was a big thud against the elevator doors, causing it to bend inward. I grabbed my chest as I tried to calm down. If I stay here any longer, I might end up having a heart attack with all these pop ups. The elevator doors open and I see Jess and Josh fighting. I mean literally fighting, nearly tearing each other apart.

"Hold up, settle down. What happened?" When I said that, Jessica backed up from pinning Josh against the wall.

"Hey Ebony. What do you mean what happened?"

"Yesterday you guys were all lovey dovey and Twilight crap, but now you guys are literally tearing each other apart." Both Josh and Jessica looked at each other and start laughing.

"What is so funny?" I asked.

"I'm sorry, Ebony. Jessica and I are good. All we were doing was training. Good job by the way, Jessica." Josh said as he gave her a kiss on the cheek. Even though her face is pale from the process of being a vampire, Jessica's face brightened up, and, if she could, blushing without the color in her face.

"Thanks. I learned from the best." she said as she smiled up at him, twirling her hair. Both of them were staring at each other, getting closer to each other.

"No, not again. Not while I am in the room... ALONE." I thought to myself. I cleared my throat, getting both of their attention.

"Hey Jess, how are you feeling?" I asked.

"I feel great. I'm getting used to my new senses and abilities. The only bad thing was waking up this morning with a slight sore neck." she said as she rubbed her neck. I looked at Josh.

"What? I said sorry." he said defensively.

"I know. I don't care. As long as I woke up next to you." she says as she hugs Josh. Oh gosh. It is kind of cute what Jessica and Josh is doing, but it is TOO cute and a little annoying. Saving me from the horror, the elevator opens and Sita, mom, and Logan got out. Logan stands beside me and smiles at me.

"Thanks for saving me from these love birds." I said quietly to him.

"Glad I could help." he said as he chuckled. I looked over at Jessica and Josh and both of them look nervous. I looked behind me to where Sita and mom are standing there. Both of them are discussing something and I could tell it was something and I could tell it was something important.

"What is going on? What happened in the elevator?" I asked Logan.

"Nothing. They didn't even say anything on the way here."

"What if they are talking about me being turned and now they want my head." Jessica said, very terrified.

"What are you talking about?" Logan asked.

"You know... the parts in the Twilight saga where newborn vampires or any vampire get their head knocked off and then burned." Josh looked confused and Logan was looking at Jessica as if she was crazy.

"They won't do anything to you, okay? You are safe. But, I have one question for you." Logan said.

"Sure."

"How many times exactly did you watch the Twilight movies?"

"Probably over 20 times. I just keep watching them because it is so awesome."

"Interesting." Logan said as he grabbed my arm and pulled me to the other side of the room."

"What?" I asked, laughing.

"And how did the both of you become best friends?" he asked. No he didn't just ask me that. I playfully hit his arm... at least I tried... as I laughed.

"What did I do?" he asked as he rubbed his arm as if it hurt.

"Yes Jessica might have her moments, but we always support each other. Just give her some time and you will probably understand her. Just get used to hearing more stuff about Twilight."

"Fine. But never leave me alone in the same room with her for a long time."

"Like I can't hear you. I'm now a vampire, remember?" Jessica yells to us.

"Jessica!" Josh, Logan, and I said.

"What did I do?... Oh." She then looked at Sita, all nervous.

"Speaking of vampires, I already know. I know a vampire when I see one. Right now I will not worry about it because we have to get enough practice done so we can be prepared tomorrow."

"I can't believe we are so close." Josh said.

"We can do this. Tomorrow, we will go into the Dark World and that would be our war grounds. Hopefully it wouldn't go so bad. We can't bring it to the real world or it will reveal our identities." Sita says.

"What about the people in the Dark World? Who will keep them safe?" I asked.

"You don't have to worry. I sent out a warning to the people. Some of them are going to a safe place and some of them even volunteered to join us."

"That's good, right? At least for us."

"Yeah. Hopefully it could make things easier for us." mom said.

"Okay, enough talking and more practice. Today we will do things differently. Logan, you stay with Josh and Jessica while Ebony will come with me and Laura." Sita says.

"You really want me to stay here? Let me remind you that I will be left here with a new born vampire, who I don't know if she fed yet, and a vampire, even though he is like a brother to me, I don't know if he would be willing to save me from his crazy girlfriend." Logan said. Jessica frowned and stuck her tongue out at him.

"You are a werewolf Logan, for Christ's sake. You know what you have to do if something bad happens." she says as mom and her start walking to the elevator.

"Good luck." I said as I got on the elevator.

"I need it. No biting okay guys because I bite back." he said as his claws stuck out of his fingertips as he walked to them.

"Please may no one hurt anyone." mom yelled to them as we got on the elevator.

"Don't worry Ms. Jenkins. Everything would be okay." Josh says as he smiles. I didn't get to see what happened next because the elevator door closed. But I did hear a faint thud as the elevator start going up. I looked at Sita and she start shaking her head and mom is rubbing her temples.

"Someone might have tripped." I said, trying to defend them, even though I know we all know it is not true.

"Yeah, okay." Sita said. The elevator door open to this room filled with at least 20 people. When we stepped out of the elevator, everyone stopped talking and looked at us. As I was following Sita and mom to the front, I hear some gasps and people whispering "Is that her?"

"Quiet down people." Sita said as she turned around to them. Mom sat in one of the chairs in the front while I sat next to her. Automatically, everyone got quiet. This wowed me on how well Sita have these people trained. My teachers at school can't even keep us quiet without threatening to give us a pop quiz on a lesson they never go through,

"Okay everyone. As you know, Laura is back, for those who have heard stories about her. And, of course, this is Ebony, if some of you were wondering. I just called you here because today we will welcome Ebony and take her in as a Legna original witch"

"Wait... what?"

Chapter 18

I was caught off guard with what just happened. For those who don't remember what happened, Sita just said that today I will become a member of the Legnas.

"We will welcome Ebony and take her in as a Legna original witch."

"Wait... what?" I thought to myself. Everyone else was clapping. I leaned over to mom.

"Mom, what is Sita talking about?"

"You are about to be accepted as a Legnas original witch. You are about to go through a ceremony where the Mothers of the Legna Witch Society will accept you."

"The what?"

"The Mothers of the Legna Witch Society. They are very powerful original witches who have died years ago. We are about to do the ritual where we would ask them to accept you as a Legna."

"So we are basically talking to the dead to get me into this Legnas thing."

"Yeah."

"Okay... you could have given me a head's up."

"I'm sorry, Ebony. I didn't have enough time."

"Okay." I said as I continued to listen to Sita.

"Ebony, I hope that's good with you?" she said.

"I'm good with what?" I am so confused right now.

"Are you okay with the ritual?"

"Of course. I would love to." I said as I forced a smile on my face. When I answered, everyone start clapping again. Sita smiled at me and turned back to the people.

"Let's begin then." Everyone got up from their seats and grabbed their chairs to line them against the walls. With the chairs gone, the room looked bigger. Everyone formed a circle around me as mom and Sita moved a table into the middle of the circle with me. The table had a candle and a knife on it. The knife caught me off guard.

"Mom, what is the knife for?" I asked, even though I kind of knew what it was for.

"I left a note on what need to be done in the ritual." she said, avoiding my question, and she and Sita got in their place within the circle. Everyone held hands as I stood alone in the circle. Mom and Sita nodded to me, telling me to start. I sighed as I looked down at the paper. There was some kind of foreign language on it that I did not understand. It almost looked like Latin. Getting nervous, I started to read it. Surprisingly, the more I read, the more I start to understand. It was like I already knew this language because I understood it and the meaning of it.

"Matres legna sagae impetrandam veniam." It means "Mothers of the Legna witches, I come with a request." The rest of the ritual was in English.

"Mothers, I have come here for a blessing. Bring me a sign that you are here." Automatically, this fire poofed out of nowhere on the candle. This wasn't any normal fire because it was like a white and blue flame. I got myself together and then I continued.

"Now with your presence, I ask of you to give me this one request. To show my commitment, the same you gave years ago, I will give a sacrifice." As I was saying this, it was as if something has taken over me. My fear and nervousness was gone. It was like a large energy filled me and I liked it. I grabbed the knife and carefully cut the palm of my hand. Blood start coming out of the wound and I squeezed my hand closed and put it over the flame. Blood drops start falling into the flame and the flame got bigger, turning the flame to a pinkish red. Next thing I know, wind came out of nowhere and start whirling around me, blowing my hair. I closed my eyes and I hear many small whispers in my head. Next thing I know, I start chanting something that I didn't know I knew. The more I chanted, the faster the wind has gotten. I hear someone yelling my name, but I ignored it and kept on going. Next thing I know, I blacked out.

I opened my eyes and I find myself surrounded in white. I was the only person here, except for the woman who was standing inches away from me. She looks so beautiful with her icy blonde hair, blue eyes, her smooth, peach skin and her long, white gown. She almost seems like an angel.

"Am I dead?" I asked, starting to panic a little.

"No, you are not dead. Right now you are having a vision." she said with her soft voice.

"Who are you?"

"I am Garcia, one of the Mothers of the Legna Witches you were asking for acceptance from. We heard your request."

"Is that why I'm here? Did I do something wrong and you guys denied my request? Why did I pass out?"

"You will know when you wake up. When you do, look at your hand and you will get your answer. About the part about you passing out, I did that. Passing out were not a part of the ritual. I made you pass out because I needed to talk to you about tomorrow." When Garcia said that, anxiety took over me. I start feeling nervous.

"Wh-What about tomorrow?"

"I am only going to say this once. What happens tomorrow doesn't end tomorrow. Someone who you knew your entire life will be lost, but then be found." Garcia said.

"What? What do you mean? Are you talking about my mom?" Garcia was confusing me so much.

"I can't say anymore. Just wake up." she said as she starts walking away.

"Wait. What does that mean?" I almost ran after her, but she was already gone. That is when I woke up.

"Ebony?" I opened my eyes and see Sita leaning over me. Mom was beside her, looking all worried as usual. Everyone else was standing all around me, staring. I hear some whispers in the group. I sat up and I had a huge migraine. I looked at the hand I cut and I saw the cut has healed, but it left a light silver scar. I touched under my nose and feel something wet, so I looked at my fingers to see blood on them. My nose was bleeding.

"What happened?" I asked as I start getting up off the floor.

"You used so much of your powers in the ritual and you lost so much energy in the process." Sita said as she helped me up and handed me tissue for my nose. That is when I remembered Garcia and what she said to me.

"Do this usually happen, passing out during the ritual and all." I said as I patted the tissue on my nose to get the blood.

"No, which is kind of weird since you are the only one who ever passed out. Maybe you used too much of you powers, more than what you needed to use."

"Maybe." I said. I could tell Sita and mom about my dream or vision or whatever they call it, but they would probably not believe me anyways. That is when I remembered.

"Hey, so how can I tell if I was accepted?"

"Let me see your hand." mom said. I gave her my hand and looked at it. That is when a smiled spread across her face.

"You were accepted. They accepted you with the silver scar. If you weren't accepted, they would have kept your wound unhealed." When mom said that, everyone start clapping for me as if I have won an award.

The elevator door opens and Logan come running out. He looked around until he looked at me and he walked up to me. He looks so concerned.

"What's wrong, Logan? Did something bad happen?" Sita asked.

"That was what I was going to ask you. Is everything all right here?"

"Why did you ask?" I asked.

"Gusts of wind came out of nowhere downstairs and I knew something went wrong."

"Well..." mom starts to say something, but I interrupted.

"Nothing. Just overuse of my powers, that's all." I did not want to tell Logan I passed out.

"But..."

"Hey Sita, are we done with the rituals?"

"Umm, yeah. So far, we are done." she said as she turned to mom looking for the final answer. Mom nodded her head. I turned to Logan.

"Logan, are you busy?"

"Well, after having to protect myself and being attacked by the vampire couple, I still have to go train my pack."

"Okay, I will go with you." his eyebrows rose when I said that.

"Umm... are you sure?"

"Yeah. Come on."

"I don't think that is a good idea." mom said.

"Don't worry mom. Everything will be alright." I said as I grabbed his arm and dragged him to the elevator. I pushed the button and turned back to the group.

"Nice to meet you guys. I had a great time until the little incident. I will see you guys later." I said. Everyone turned and waved goodbye. They are so quiet... my type of group. I turned back around and got on the elevator with Logan and waved at them as the elevator door closed. Mom was the only one who was not smiling. I turned to Logan and he was shaking his head with a little grin on his face.

"What?"

"What is the real reason for you wanting to hang around me?"

"What are you talking about?"

"You want to hang around me and other werewolf guys, knowing how nervous you get with just me around."

"I do not okay. I just kind of got embarrassed in there and I can't stay knowing they seen me embarrass myself. That is all I got to say about it." I confessed.

"What happened in there?"

"Don't worry about it. How did things go with Jessica and Josh?" I asked, changing the subject. When I asked this, he automatically frowned.

"Don't even remind me. As soon as the elevators doors closed, they became monsters. Both of the, tackled me to the elevator door. I thought getting into my wolf form would help me, but it made no difference. Your little blonde friend Jessica decided it was alright to grab my tail and throw me across the room while Josh did nothing to stop her. It took all of me not to tear both of them apart. You need to talk to her." I didn't say anything for a while because I was trying to keep myself from laughing.

"Are you alright now?" I tried to give him a comforting smile, but his serious face did not bulge.

"What do you think?"

"I'm guessing not."

"My body was sore afterwards, but I healed so it doesn't hurt anymore. But, I am still pissed, so keep both of those bloodsuckers away from me." That is when I couldn't hold the laughter in any longer. I start laughing and I knew this made Logan even madder.

"That is not even funny."

"I'm so sorry. I just can't help it."

"Yeah, okay. At least I can get you to smile." he said as he gave me his famous smile I love so much. I couldn't help blushing and

113

smiling. I turned my face away. Next thing I know, he is holding my hand, our fingers intertwined. I turned to him and looked into his blue eyes. My heart is doing the same irregular heartbeats it does whenever I'm with Logan.

"Ebony, I have something to ask you." Before he got the chance to ask, the elevator door opened to this open field with a few trees. This broke the trance and we let go of each other's hand. There was no one out here. We got out of the elevator and I kept looking around for wolves or shirtless guys, but I didn't see anyone.

"I though you said you were coming here to train you pack. I don't see anyone."

"Just wait. One of them do the same thing every training."

"Do what?" Before he got to answer, out of nowhere, someone tackled Logan. They went flying into the tree beside me, causing it to fall.

"This." Logan said as he groaned. I covered my mouth, in shock and trying not to laugh. The guy who tackled Logan got off of Logan and helped him up.

"Hey Logan." he said as he patted Logan on his back. The guy looked at me and smiled.

"Well, hello. We didn't know we were having any guests." he said.

"Dereck, where is the rest of the pack?" Logan asked as he rubbed his back. I hear something and I turned to see five more guys with only pants on coming to us. The sixth person coming was a girl.

"Wow, a girl werewolf." I thought to myself.

"What took you so long? We were starting to think you ditched us." One of the guys said.

"Sorry. I had to help the vampire Legnas. We had a new member and they needed a toy. Apparently, that was me."

"Don't forget the part about that Ebony chick." Dereck said.

"Aren't you going to introduce us?" the girl said, all hyper. She's pretty with her smooth, lightly tanned face, black hair, and brown eyes. She looks so sweet, which is kind of surprising since she is basically a fighter.

"How can I forget? Ebony, this is my crazy pack. As you know, that is Dereck. He is known for being the jokester of the group." Logan said as he pointed to Dereck.

"Hey, I don't always make jokes. Speaking of which..."

"We don't care. The guy next to him is Jake. He is the quiet and sensitive one, but he can fight very well."

"Hi, I'm not that sensitive." Jake said as he waved and smiled at me.

"Yeah right. When you found me and your sister together you quickly punched me in the face and ended up breaking my nose, even though we were doing nothing." Dereck said.

"I apologized. You know I'm protective of my little sister. Besides, you were trying to touch her butt."

"I was getting something off of it." Dereck said as he chuckled. Before Jake got to reply, Logan interrupted their argument.

"Back to the introducing. The guy next to Jake is Conner. He is kind of dull and boring, but at least I can count on him in doing his job. Both of you might actually get along." Logan said as he looked over at me and smiled. I just rolled my eyes.

"I'm not boring. I know how to have fun."

"No Connor." the girl said, shaking her head.

"What about that time we went to the club and I made a fool of myself on the dance floor."

"You were drunk."

"No I wasn't. I didn't drink that day."

"Well..." she didn't get to finish because she start to giggle.

"You spiked my drinks?" Connor looked so mad.

"You were saying, Logan?" she said as she turned back to him.

"You are wrong Alina. I knew something was wrong with him that night." Logan said as he tried not to laugh. The other guys in the pack didn't bother holding there's in.

"What? He was so dry, I had to do something." she said.

"Next is Grant. He is the baby and new to this pack." Grant looks no older than 15.

"Hi." he says as he waves shyly at me,

"Hi."

"The last guy in the group is Xavier, Grant's older brother. I suggest you stay away from him." Logan said.

"Why?" I asked. A smile spread over Xavier's face.

"Just ignore him. Nice to meet you, Ebony." he said as he stuck his hand out. I thought he wanted a handshake so I gave him my hand, but as soon as I did, he pulled me- no, more like yanked me- to him.

"He doesn't deserve you." he whispered. Logan grabbed my other arm and pulled me away from Xavier.

"Stop it." Logan growled at him.

"What? I was just kidding." Logan just frowned at him and turned to me. As soon he did, Xavier mouths "No I'm not" and winks at me.

"Just ignore him."

"Xavier, you see she's already taken. Just leave her alone." Grant said to him. When he was saying this, Xavier wasn't even paying attention. He was too busy mocking Grant.

"Just shut up." Xavier said as he shoved him.

"Don't touch me." Grant said as he shoved him back. Next thing I know, both of them are about to attack each other, but Logan push both of them away from each other, sending both of them across the field.

"Not today, okay guys." Logan said to them.

"Yes." both of them said as they both got off of the ground, brushing themselves off.

"Thank you. Now to finish, the last person in our pack and the only female in it is Alina. I don't have to tell you much about her because she shows it." Alina jumps up and down and go up to me and hugs me.

"I can tell we would be best friends!" she says, but neither I nor the others were paying attention to her. We were too busy paying attention to Grant and Xavier, who both ran to each other. Next thing you know, they jump at each other and they transformed to their wolf forms. Everyone backed away and Logan pushed me back.

"Aren't you guys going to stop them?" I asked.

"Don't worry. They do this at every practice." Logan said as he took off his shoes and shirt. Next thing I know, Logan is running towards them and he turned to his wolf form too. He bit down on Xavier's tail and flung him across the field. Xavier got off the ground and start running towards Logan, as if he was going to attack him. Logan got into his attack position, turned to Xaiver and growled at him real loud. Xavier backed down and whined. Logan turned to Grant and Grant was already backing down, whining. He looks so scared. I looked around at the other pack members to see how they were reacting to this, but their facial expressions has not changed since before all of this. It was like they are used to it. How was I reacting? Well, just to let you know, I'm hiding behind Alina. I know it's sad, but I can't help it if I am scared so don't judge me.

Chapter 19

Logan turns around as if he is looking for someone. He keeps looking until he looked directly at me. It look like he was sad, but I can't really tell with him in his wolf form. He transformed out of his wolf form and turned to his pack.

"Now, does anyone else want to fight today? This is our last day to practice before Venomar and his Nomeds. This is a life and death situation, so we need to stop all these childish actions and work on making sure we can kick ass tomorrow."

"We're ready." the pack said.

"Let's get to work then." That's when everyone got into their wolf form, except for Logan. The pack then starts teaming up.

"What are you doing? Don't you need to be in your wolf form to communicate with them?" I asked Logan as I stood next to him.

"I can communicate with them telepathically. Also, if I want, I can just talk to them and they will respond through their mind."

"That's interesting." I said as I turned to look at him. That's when I noticed he still didn't have his shirt on, so his bare chest was showing. I turned away as I felt myself starting to blush. I picked up his shirt from off the floor and gave it to him.

"Can you please put your shirt on?"

"Why?" he said as he smiled at me.

"Because, it's kind of distracting me." I said as I kept my head turned away from him.

"Take a good look if you want. I really don't mind."

"Just put on the shirt please."

"Fine, I'll do it. You don't have to beg."

"You wish." I said as I gave him his shirt. As soon as he put it on, I hear the elevator door open. I turn to see Josh, Jessica, and a group of other people getting off and walking towards us. Logan, looking confused, walked to him.

"Hey, Logan." Josh said as he smiled.

"Hey. Um, what are you guys doing here? Did something happen?"

"No. Sita gave me a call and told me that she want us to practice together. She tried reaching you, but you weren't answering your phone."

"Fine, I'll go tell the pack." Logan said as he walked away to his pack. Jessica walks up to me with a huge smile on her face.

"What's with the smile on your face, Jess?" I said as I chuckled.

"I'm just so excited. We get to spend some time with each other. With all of this stuff happening and me turning, we barely see each other."

"I know. We just have to be patient and soon things will be somewhat normal again." I said. I was trying to pay full attention to Jessica, but I was too busy looking behind her at Josh and the other people.

"Um, who are the other people with you guys?"

"Oh, they are the other vampires that are a part of the Legnas. They are all cool so don't worry."

Logan came to me smiling.

"Now I need a favor from you." he said. I raised an eyebrow at him.

"That depends on what it is." I said.

"I want you to be our damsel and distress." he smiled.

Before I could say anything, out of nowhere, Josh came and grabbed me.

"What are you doing?" I asked him.

"Just hang on." he said. Before I could ask why, he quickly put me on his back and start running. I start screaming as his speed start picking up.

"Put me down." I screamed. I had to close my eyes to keep the wind from getting in. A few minutes later, I opened my eyes and see that Josh was climbing up a tree.

"Oh god." I said as I held on him tightly. I can hear Josh chuckling. He stopped on the top branch and sat me down. I hugged the tree.

"What the hell, Josh?! Why are we up here?"

"Wait and see."

"Josh, if you don't tell me..." Next thing I know, one of the werewolves jumped out of one of the trees and tackled Josh off the tree.

"Oh crap." I said as I look down. I couldn't even see the ground. I whimpered and held on the tree tightly. Jessica came to me smiling.

"Hey Ebony." she said.

"Don't 'hey' me. What is going on down there?" I said. A wolf jumped at Jessica, but she punches it in the face and threw it down. She looked back at me.

"You are our damsel and distress."

"I know that but why am I on top of a tree?"

"Don't ask me. I don't know why Josh put you up here." A wolf tackled Jessica off the branch. Then the wolf turns back to me and transformed. It was Alina. She smiles and come to me.

"Sorry I had to tackle your friend like that."

"No problem. Can you tell me what is going on?"

"Well we are fighting to get to you. We have to get you to the elevator to safety. Whoever does win."

"You'll are crazy. What do you mean safely?" All Alina did was smile as she transformed back to a wolf. She leaned back down and leaped to a different branch.

"Where are you going? Aren't you going to get me down from here?" She jumped down from the branch. I looked down to see if I see her, but I didn't. I groaned. I need to get down from here. Out of nowhere, Logan came down, landing in front of me.

"You ok?" he asked.

"Do I look okay? I'm stuck up here."

Logan chuckled. "I know."

"It's not funny."

"I know. Sorry about that, but it is really not my fault."

"How is it not your fault?"

"Well, you wanted to come. So here you are."

"I didn't expect this!"

"I know I know."

"If you know, then get me down from here."

"Say please." He smiles.

"Can you get me down from here? Please!" I yelled at him. A smile spread across his face.

"That's what I plan to do." he said as he quickly grabbed me and put me over his shoulder.

"Hey! Put me down!" I yelled as I hit his back but he didn't listen. He just jumped down from the tree. I screamed as I closed my eyes. Have I ever mentioned that I am afraid of heights?

"What the hell I got myself into." I yelled as Logan was running me to safety.

"This is not even half of it. Hold on." Logan said as he laughed to what I said. That's when I noticed the last thing Logan said.

"Wait, what do you mean hold on?" After I said that, out of nowhere, one of the vampires in Josh's group attacked Logan to the ground from behind. Let me remind you, I'm still hanging over Logan's shoulder. Ouch!

Chapter 20

"Ebony, I'm so sorry about your ankle." Logan said as he places me gingerly on the couch. Jessica went to the freezer and grabbed an ice pack.

"Oh it's no problem. It's not like I have a sprained ankle from you falling on it. It's no problem at all, even though I have to defeat a powerful and don't forget, experienced, maniac who wants me dead. It's just no problem at all." I snapped at him. Logan looked like he wanted to laugh but he held it in.

"The sarcasm was not really necessary." he says.

"It was pretty fun though, the practice." Jessica says as she walks over to me and placed the ice pack on my now swollen ankle. I winced in pain.

"Look on the bright side. If James attacked Logan from the front, instead of the back, your ankle wouldn't have been the one landed on. At least you still have your pretty face, in other words." Alina says, in her same hyper voice. Logan looked at her until her smile disappeared and she backed down.

"I'm just saying. Sorry for me trying to lighten up the mood." she said, almost in a whimper.

"Thank you, Alina." I spoke up and gave her a smile. That's when her grin came back. You hear the elevator door open and Josh comes out.

"How is everything?" He asked as he walked into the living room and sat next to Jessica.

"Everything's good. Nothing was broken at least." Logan says.

""Well just to let you know, Sita and Laura heard about what happened so don't be surprised if they come in..." Before Josh got to finish, the elevator doors opened and Sita and mom comes running into the room with Izzy running in after them.

"Right now." Josh continued as he chuckled. They ran over to my side and Sita kneeled beside me. Mom just bent down and hugged me, looking concerned.

"Ebony, are you okay?" she asked, all worried.

"Mom, I am fine. You guys are acting like I died or something," I said as I pushed her away.

"All I know is that I hear people talking, saying there was a horrible accident that occurred during the training for the werewolves and vampires. Then we hear your name so we ran up here." Mom said as she straightened up.

"What happened?" Sita said as she shot a look at Logan.

"Why are you looking at me?!?" he said, getting all defensive.

"Because, I put you in charge of looking after Ebony, yet now here she is on the couch, injured."

"Don't worry, she only have a sprained ankle. Also I tried to protect her. It's just this time I was a little too late."

"Don't go on him. It was an accident and we can't go back in time and take it back." I said as I looked up at Logan and gave him a small smile. He smiled back,

"Well, since it is a sprained ankle, I think I can do something to heal you so you don't have any interference at the battle tomorrow." She pulled out this small pouch that was connected to her belt. Sita look so beautiful today with her long blonde hair out, cascading down her back and she had on a navy blue v neck sweater on with some jeans.

She pulled out some of this powder like substance out and rubbed it in her hands. Logan removed the ice pack from my foot and Sita picked up my foot gently as she chanted something.

"Powers of the Legna witches come to me. Give me the powers that right now I so do need. Healing powers in this substance I bind to thee, where I lay my hands, so healed will it be. And if more power this spell may need, may the Mothers of the Legna witches then, as they wish, intercede"

She rubbed my ankles and closed her eyes as she continued to chant. Next thing I know, I feel a tingly sensation in my ankle and the pain starts to subside. After she was done, she laid my foot back down and put the ice pack back on it.

"What was that?" I asked, all surprised.

"It's one of the healing spells. You should know this since you're reading the spell book." she said as she got up. I broke eye contact with her, feeling embarrassed.

"Uhh yeah, I remember." I said as I laughed nervously.

"Sure. Well just to 'remind you,' I just used a healing spell. The powder substance is alder leaves grinded up. This is supposed to take away pain and make the swelling subside. By tomorrow, your foot should be healed but I don't want you moving around. The chant is what put the herbs to work. Of course you know that already, right?" Sita said as she smiled at me. I could hear Jessica chuckle and I glared at her. Her smile disappeared as fast as it came.

"Now Ebony, I don't want you leaving that couch today. Even though your foot is healed, we don't want to take any chances. Venomar is coming tomorrow and we can't take any chances, especially when he is after you, trying to kill you." mom said.

"But mom, what am I supposed to do on this couch?" I whined.

"Learn the spell book because I know you didn't finish it."

"What? Of course I read it. I don't know what you're talking about. But I will study more, if you insist." I said quickly.

"Good. Well we have to leave now. There is a meeting we have to attend but if you need me, you know where to find me." Mom said her and Sita walked over to the elevator.

I groaned. "Oh fine. Go to your meeting." Mom kissed me on my forehead.

"Study." Mom said as her and Sita got on the elevator. As soon as the elevator closed, I threw a pillow at Logan.

"What I do?" Logan said as he laughed.

"Because of you, I have to stay on this stupid couch." I threw another pillow at him again, but this time he caught it. Jessica came to me and sat on the arm of the couch.

"Don't worry, we will help you study." Jessica said

"We??" Josh and Logan said at the same time. Jessica growled.

"Yes. We are not leaving my best friend here by herself, especially you Logan since you are the one who hurt her ankle."

"She is right. You hurt our best friend. We all need to help Ebony study and beat Venomar." Alina said as she stood beside Jessica. Jessica looked over at Alina, looking all confused.

"Our best friend? Um Ebony, who is this?" she said as she looked at Alina up and down.

"Oh hi!!! You must be Jessica, Ebony's best friend. I'm Alina and I just met Ebony today but we just clicked and we are like best friends now. So I guess that makes us best buddies too. We might as well so yay!!!" She said as she hugged Jessica, jumping up and down.

"Yay!" Jessica said as she gave the fakest giggle I ever heard her give. She backed away from Alina and stood closer to me, mumbling.

"I don't like how hyper she is."

"She's just like you. You are just as hyper as she is." I whispered back.

"Exactly my point. There don't need to be two Jessicas. I'm already awesome as it is." She said as she flipped her hair and smiled at me. That is when both of us start laughing.

"Oh Jessica. You are so funny." Alina said as she playfully punched her in the arm before she walked to the kitchen. Jessica shot her a look but quickly smiled again. As we started, Logan frowned, not looking forward to that all-nighter, and sat down on a chair while Josh sat on the other chair. Isabella laid down on the love seat and end up falling asleep while everyone else help me study. Jessica, Alina, and Logan end up falling asleep later on so Josh was the only one helping me. Josh smooth his hair back as he turns to the next page.

"This is so freaking hard. How much did we go through so far?" I said

"Half of the book. I'm so happy I'm a vampire." He said as he lean back. I threw a pillow at him. "No offense."

"Too late." Josh sat up and threw the pillow back at me. I laughed.

"I don't want to study anymore. Is there a spell in the book that makes me receive all the information from this big book?" Josh looks through the book for no more than 5 minutes, using his speed.

"Nope."

I groaned. "I'm not staying on this stupid couch all day."

"You supposed to be resting."

"I don't want to. I want to get up and do something. I want to go home and live a normal life. I want my Justin back. I don't want to wake up in the morning and find out that I might die in this war." I didn't realize I was crying until Josh handed me tissue and sat down beside me.

"Ebony, don't stress yourself out about this."

"Josh, how am I not supposed to be stressed? How would you feel if Isabella was killed by a lunatic and you find out that you are this powerful witch who have to go through battle and might die in the process?" Josh wraps his arms around me and gave me a hug while I cried.

"I would feel devastated, but I would deal with it because I know that a lot of people are depending on me. Ebony, the war is tomorrow whether if you like or not. This is your responsibility."

"I'm so scared."

"We are all scared, but we are all a family. We stick together. We fight together. That's all that matters."

"What if I fail? Then I would let you all down or... my brother. What if I die?" Josh turns my head for I am look right at him

"Enough with the 'what if's.' Don't worry about letting anyone down. Just go into battle tomorrow knowing that you are fighting for something right. No matter if you win or die. Okay?" I sniffed and nodded my head.

"Now I know why Jess fell for you. You are great with words." Josh laughed.

"Thanks. Now I know why you and Jess are best friends." Before I could say anything, Isabella starts screaming. Logan and Alina sat up straight in alert while Jessica ends up falling off her chair. Josh went over to Isabella and tried to calm her down, but she pushed him away. Isabella got up quickly and was in front of me instantly.

"He's coming." She said. Isabella was shaking.

"Who's coming?" I asked. She grabbed my shirt as she starts crying.

"He's coming. Call Sita now!" she yells. Logan grabs Isabella's shoulders and turns her towards him.

"Who, Isabella? You have to tell us the person that is coming." he asked. The power went off.

"Venomar is here." She says silently.

Chapter 21

"Who Isabella? You have to tell us the person that is coming." he asked. The power went off.

"Venomar is here." She says silently. As soon as she said that, I felt chills running down my spine.

"Wait, I thought he wasn't supposed to arrive until tomorrow. Why is he here now?" I asked, my voice raised and scared. The alarm starts to go off.

"We need to get out of here." Logan said as he quickly picked up Isabella. Alina helped me stand up and we all went into the elevator. My heart start beating faster as I realized that this battle has just became reality.

"You girls stay behind us as soon as we get out. We don't know who could have made it in here and roaming the hallways right now." Logan said as he handed Isabella to me. As soon as the elevator door opens, Logan starts leading us slowly out the elevator. Jessica and Alina stood on both side of me. Josh was standing behind me. Isabella starts to whimper and she held tightly to me as we were walking down the hallway. I couldn't believe that this was happening right now. I tried to stay calm for Izzy, but my heart was racing. I'm not ready for this. Venomar must really want me dead if he is doing this war now. The alarm is going off so loud. As soon as we turned the corner, two guys attacked Logan to the ground. They look like the same men who attacked at the school. Isabella screamed and Jessica and Alina moved us back. Josh pulled one of the men off of Logan. As soon as Logan was up, he looks so angry. With his hands down, his claws automatically came out his fingertips and he start tearing into one of the guys' throat. The guy dropped down on the floor, blood gushing out of the wound, and now dead. Josh hands start to glow a whitish blue as he lifted his hands and put one hand on the other guy's head as he stood up. The man starts screaming in agony.

"What is happening?" I asked.

"Josh is bringing pain to him." Alina said. The man fell to his knees as blood start coming from his mouth, nose, and ears. Isabella hid behind my hair as I closed my eyes. After a few seconds, it was quiet. All I can hear is the alarm. I open my eyes and see the two guys laying there lifeless. Logan was back to his normal self, but he still had blood on his shirt.

"We need to hurry out of here. Now." Josh said. So we all ran down the hall until we get to this huge room, which was full. The lights were dim with red lights and everyone was panicking. Mom and Sita were trying to calm everyone. I put Isabella down and walked up to Mom and Sita.

"The war wasn't supposed to start today! Both of you lied!" I yelled.

"Ebony, please calm down." Mom said

"No! Venomar wasn't supposed to be here. He's doing this on purpose. He really wants me dead so badly." I said as tears start running down my cheek.

"It was supposed to start tomorrow. We had everything planned." Sita said.

"Oh really. Then you are not doing a pretty good job. It seems more like the war is happening right now." I said angrily.

"Ebony watch your mouth right now. We know you are scared right now, but you don't have to be disrespectful."

"I'm sorry. I'm just not ready." Mom walked up to me and gave me a hug as I cried.

"Now Ebony, I need you to stop crying right now." Mom said as she wiped the tears from my face as she looked me in my eyes. She looks so serious right now. That's when I noticed that mom's clothes and hair were soaking wet. I breathed slowly as I tried to calm down.

"Are you calm now?" She asked.

"Unfortunately, yes but mom, what happened to you?"

"We went outside to see what had happened, causing the alarm to go off, and it turns out that it is pouring down raining outside. But ignore all of that. Now I know you do not want to hear this but you have to stay strong. We all were caught by surprise and apparently Venomar is here now. We cannot do anything about that but we can calm down and do what we can do best, which is defeat Venomar."

"Okay. I'm sorry. I got this." Mom smiled at me as she turns around when someone taps her on her shoulder.

"Mrs. Jenkins, we can't seem to get the computer for surveillance to turn back on. Power is off all around the building there is nothing else I can do to make this computer turn back on."

"That's what I thought. Well thank you Chris for the update. I can take it from here." Mom said as she walked over to the computer. People moved out of her way as she stood in front of the computer. I don't know what she is about to do but I never really know anything anymore. Mom stood in front of the computer and I watched as she took a deep breath and lifted her hands towards the screen. She looked so focused on what she was doing, which I really didn't know what it was. I haven't really finished the book. After a while, the computer came on and everyone started cheering.

"Everyone, there is no time for us to be cheering. We still need to look at the surveillance cameras to see where Venomar's people are roaming around." Sita said as she shushed them. Chris got back on the computer and he start doing what he needed to do to get the surveillance cameras to turn on. Next thing I know, there are four different screen scenes. Chris kept moving through different camera shots until he found what he was looking for, the camera that was showing Jessica and my room. More of Venomar's men and surprisingly some women were in there, throwing furniture, pulling away doors, and tearing at the walls. The screen then changed to a camera in my room and there were more of Venomar's people in there. My bed was already turned over and everything else was a mess. Next thing I know, I see one of the guys and one of the girls picking up some of my clothes, pulled it up to their face and start sniffing them. Out of nowhere, another guy walked in. stopped, looked right at the camera and smiled. This guy is different from the other people because this guy was wearing a cloak, unlike the other ones. That's when all I was looking now was the snow screen on the computer. I don't know if it was just me, but I automatically got cold all over.

"Damn." Sita said as she turned away from the computer,

"What just happened? What were they doing?" I asked, getting even more scared. Sita looked over at Logan.

"Logan, I want you to take Ebony somewhere safe. Make sure you take her near any moist areas that would help take away her scent. Josh, I want you to take your sister somewhere quiet and secrete so she can be safe. I don't want her seeing any of this. After that, get your group prepared" Sita says.

"Okay." Josh says as he grabs her from me and starts to leave.

"And Josh?"

"Yes Sita?"

"Just in case, tell Izzy how much you love her."

134

"Of course I will." He said as he pulled Isabella closer to him and swiftly ran out of the room. Sita turned back to Logan.

"The same goes to you too, Logan. After you drop Ebony off, I want you to go to your pack and prepare them. Alina and Jessica, both of you go to your groups. Everyone else, you know what to do. Now go."

"Yes Sita" Everyone said all at once, besides me.

"No. I'm not leaving until someone tells me what just happened. What were those people doing in the suite?" I asked, trying to be demanding but I know I failed at that, knowing how scared I was so I know it showed. Sita sighed and looked me dead into my eyes.

"Ebony, as you know, those were Venomar's men and since they are in your suite, it shows that they are looking for you. You can tell that some of them were werewolves because two of them were just sniffing some of your clothes to get your scent, which is why I am making Logan send you somewhere moist, anywhere with water, because water will mask your scent, keeping them from finding you. But, the longer you stay here, the more time it give them to come and find you and we do not want that, especially since we just found out that they have witch on their side. The man in the cloak must be Venomar's personal witch, who must have found a way for his men to get in here. Now all I want you to do is just trust me Ebony and do what I say because I am trying to save you but only if you let me." Sita said, as her voice was raising more and more as she was talking.

"I'm so sorry. Of course I can do that." I said, almost speechless.

"Thank you." She said as she tried to give me a smile, but her being worried took over. That's when Logan grabbed my hand and took me back to the elevator. As soon as the doors closed, I looked over to Logan to see how he was handling all of this but his facial expression was blank.

I wanted to say something to him but I don't know how he would react so I didn't say anything. The elevator doors opened to Logan's home and he led me to closer to the waterfall.

"Now I want you to stay right here. I will be back as soon as I can, Make sure you stay in this exact spot, not anywhere else because we are not trying to take any more chances for them to find you. Also, you would need this. It gets really cold in here at night." he said as he gave me a jacket.

"I'm guessing you are about to leave." I said as I put it on and looked at him.

"Yeah, I have to. You heard Sita's orders. Don't worry. I'll be back as soon as I can before you know it." He said as he starts walking back to the direction of the elevator.

"Logan, wait." He turned around as I ran to him and gave him a hug. I can tell he was caught by surprise but he hugged me back. I backed up after a while and cleared my throat.

"Sorry, I did that just in case I might not see you again after you leave." I said as I gave him a small smile. A smile spreads across his face.

"Well in that case, I have something better." He said as he touched my cheek and kissed me. After that, he brushed a strand of hair out of my face.

"By the way, this will not be the last time you see me." He said as he smiled and walked away.

"I hope you're right," I said quietly as I sat down on the ground. I am so confused right now. I don't know if I am prepared for any of this that is happening. I thought I was going to be prepared but I didn't know it was going to be this soon. Everyone is fighting to keep me alive. Some of them might die because of me. All because of me. I never wanted this to happen. I didn't ask for these powers. I wished I didn't have them. I broke down in tears as I start to freak out. Why can't the world be a happy place? Why can't I change my own destiny? I don't want this war to happen. I lay down on the ground shaking. I closed my eyes and start humming to myself a melody that I would hum to Justin. I hummed until I drift off to sleep.

****

I wake up and I'm still in Logan's forest or I think I am. Am I dreaming? If I am, this is definitely not a good time to be doing that. I looked around until I stopped at a figure of a person in the shadows, watching me. Okay Ebony, stay calm. It is just a dream. Whoever it is can't hurt me.

"Who are you?" I asked. The person didn't even say anything. I couldn't help but to look away and tried to walk away. When I turned around, Garcia from my vision before came. I almost screamed, but she stopped me by covering my mouth with her hand.

"I'm going to make this quick. You don't have much time. I know you are scared right now, but you have a choice." She said. She let go of my mouth and start backing up.

"What you mean I have a choice? Choice of what?" She was about to say something, but I woke up to someone grabbing me. I swung at the person in the face. I can tell the guy was The a vampire with his really pale skin and his grip on me was cold. I stood up and face him. I held out my hand and did a chant until my hand lit. I threw the fire at him, but he ducked every time. He smiled with satisfaction as he tried grabbing me, but I duck out the way. I grabbed a branch and broke it off the tree. I ran to him and tried to stake him in his heart, but I missed it. The guy groaned in pain and took the branch out his chest. I tried to run, but the next thing I know, someone hit from

137

behind. I blacked out instantly. This is definitely not a dream and this person actually did hurt me.

Chapter 22

I wake up as I felt the sunlight hitting my face. I opened my eyes as I looked around to see my surroundings. I am in a four wall corridor with brownish walls, which I can tell is not supposed to be that color. That's when I noticed that I am not in Logan's forest anymore and I remembered everything that happened last night.

"Oh no, I was kidnapped last night." I thought to myself as I quickly sat up. Oh how I quickly regret it as I felt a sharp pain in the back of my head. I never had such a horrible migraine ever. I touched the back of my head and felt a knot, which I was kind of happy about since it wasn't any open wounds. I look and see the door to the room. I have to get out of here. I hope Sita and the others are looking for me. I got up slowly from the floor and walked over to the door. What I found oddly strange was that there was a door knob on the inside where I am. Either Venomar is not as intelligent as everyone thought he was or there is this terrible reason for why this knob is on this door. Well, there is only one way to find out. I slowly grabbed the doorknob and turned it and that is when I got my answer. A quick shock went through the doorknob into me. I quickly let go and rubbed my sore hands. Well I guess it was not meant for me to let myself out.

"Hello! Can anyone hear me!!! Please let me out of here and I won't hurt you!!!" I yelled. Next thing I know, I hear locks and chains coming off so I backed away from the door. One of Venomar's men comes into the room with a smug smile on his face.

"You? Hurt me? I don't think so sweetheart. I heard all about you, rookie. You might be as powerful as people say you are but you sure don't know how to use them yet."

"You are right. I'm guessing you think you can beat me in a heartbeat."

"I think? Listen girl, I suggest you shut your mouth right now or I will shut it for you before Venomar come take his turn." He said as he snarled at me.

"If I'm as weak as you say I am, what were those chains and locks for? Also, the electrocuting door knobs, what is the purpose of those?" he almost responded but he closed his mouth. I smiled when I knew I had him.

"Also, I am going to take one more guess at this. I'm guessing when Venomar told you about me, he also gave you orders to never open this door just in case. But you, being as cocky as I'm guessing you always been, you decide that you can handle me all by yourself."

"Shut up!" he yelled.

"One thing you didn't know is that this rookie have been practicing her spells so the powers I supposedly don't know how to use, I do know how to use and very well." That's when he snapped and I saw his claws come out his fingers, which was really the only thing I was surprised of because I didn't read that from him. When he started to pounce at me, everything seems to be going in slow motion. As soon as he got up in the air, I used one of the spells I read in the book. I lifted my hands towards him and he froze like he was supposed to. As I smiled, I swiftly moved my hand down to the wall. That is when he was thrown hard to the wall and fell. Next thing you know, he start screaming in agonizing pain. You already know what's happening right now.

"Okay, please stop." He cries out. I put my hand down and smiled in satisfaction. He looked up at me and growled.

"You… you…" he tried to talk as he tried to get up but I lifted my hands again and he starts screaming again in pain. He starts shaking and then he was still. Well I can't exactly say he's going to wake up feeling wonderful. I wiped off my hands and stepped over him as I walked out of the room. I have to hurry out of here before I find another idiot like him. As I walked down the hallway, I made sure I was listening for any footsteps. I turned the corner and saw an elevator. I sighed in relief as I pushed the down button. The elevator doors opened and I got on. As it was going down, I went to the corner and sat down as I tried to relax. Next thing I know, I screamed as I hear a thud on the top of the elevator. Someone pulls the door that lets you in on top and two men and a woman jumped in. I screamed as they tried to grab for me but then someone else jumps in through the top. Next thing I know mom turns around and punched the first guy in the face and elbowed the second one in his chest. She then swiftly pulled out a gun and shot the woman three times in the heart. She then shot the two men in the head, moving from one to the other, moving back and forth. After she was done, she stuck the gun back in the back of her pants. She then turned to me and smiled. I slowly got off the floor and brushed myself off.

"Are you okay Ebony? Are you hurt?"

"Um, I just have a small knot on the back of my head from when they knocked me out last night but I'm okay. Mom, where did all of that come from? How did you find me?" I asked as I hugged her.

"A lot of experience and mother's instinct, of course."

"Mom. Seriously."

"We tracked you down with the blood that was left on the knife from your ceremony. It's a long story but we have to leave now. As soon as the elevator reached the ground level, we ran out of the building and I stopped as I saw the scene that was taking place right now. We are not in the Dark World anymore. We are in the regular world.

"Mom, I thought the war is supposed to happen in the Dark World?"

"Yeah, Venomar can be really sneaky. Apparently, he wants to make a show over here so we have to find him before this go on any further." I look back in front of me as I saw that we were right in front of an open field that was across the street from the town. People were holding their phones up, recording what they probably thought was a show for them. What they didn't know was that right in front of us was the war itself. I see Logan and his pack tearing up Venomar's pack and Josh with his group fighting Venomar's vampires. The Legna witches' clan is fighting the Nomed clan.

"Mom, how long have this war been going on?"

"All night." Mom replied.

"Where is Sita?" Before I get to answer, an electrical pole that was on fire was coming our way. Sita got in front of us and held up her hands, making it stop. Her face showed struggle as she moved both of her hands to an area with some of Venomar's people were standing and the electrical pole landing on top of them, burning them alive. Sita turned to us, breathing a little heavy.

"Are you okay?" I asked her.

"Don't worry about me. The heavier the object is, the more power you have to use, that's all. Are you okay? Logan comes to us, telling us that you were missing when he went back to check on you." Sita says as she swiftly took out her gun, turned and shot the girl that was about to attack her from behind.

"Wooden bullets. They help when you're about to get attacked by vampires." She said as she smiled. Next thing I know Jessica and Josh lands in front of me and Logan, in his wolf form, jumps in front of me.

"Oh my gosh Ebony. I am so happy that you are alright." She said as she gave me a big hug.

"I'm happy to be alright but Jess, can you let go of me. I can't breathe." I said in barely a whisper.

"I'm sorry. I almost forgot that I am a vampire now." She said as she let go of me and backed away. Logan walks up to me and whimpered. I rubbed his face as he looked in my eyes as pushed his face closer to my palm.

"Looks like someone else is happy to see you." Josh says as he laughed. Out of nowhere, we can hear the sirens of police cars, which interrupted Josh's laugh. From a distance, I see the cars driving in our direction.

"Darn, this was something I was trying to avoid." Sita says as she ran towards the car, killing Venomar's people who got in the way. Jessica, Logan, mom, and Josh followed her so I did too. Sita stopped in front of the police car and used her powers to lift the car. That's when Josh got in front of her and grabbed the front of the car. Sita stepped back as Josh pushed the car back away from the war and put it back down. We ran to the side of the car and Sita walked up. The police officers looked terrified when we approached them.

"I'm sorry sir but its best if you stay away from that area." She said in a kind voice.

"What is going on? Who are you?" The driver asked, all terrified.

"For your own safety, don't ask any questions and just tell your squad to just ignore all of this and drive away."

"How can we ignore it." That's when the police officers looked behind us and saw Logan in his huge wolf form, growling.

"Um, second thoughts, I think we will leave." The police officer said as he spun his car around and drove away. I guess the police officer made the call because that's when the other police cars turned around and followed him.

"Okay, we got one problem out of the way." Sita says.

"You still have me!!!" we all hear a voice yell from the field. We all turned around as we see the bodies' filled field. The Legna people were standing to the side and we see Venomar standing in the middle of the field with two people in a cloak. One of them was really short.

"Venomar, we defeated most of your people. Why don't you just give up right now and we call it truce." Sita yells to him.

"No. I will not leave until I get what I came here for. I want Ebony over here now."

"Just leave us alone!" mom yells but I touched her arm to get her attention.

"Mom, I got this." She turned to me with tears in her eyes.

"But Ebony…."

"Mom, he's never going to stop if we don't do this now. It either happens now or later."

"Ebony, you don't have to do this." Jessica says as she steps up.

"I know but I choose to do this for myself and these people." As I said that, I remembered what

Garcia said in my dream earlier. This is what she meant. After that, I turned back to Venomar and start walking to him. The people of the town moved out of my way. Next thing I know, I'm standing a few feet away from him. I looked behind me and see Sita, mom, Josh, Jessica and Logan, in his human form, standing to the side, a few feet away from me. I smiled at them as I turned back to him.

"You have me here now, Venomar." I said.

"That's fabulous. I knew you were going to make it out of the building. You're a fighter just like your mother….. and just like your brother."

"Is that all you wanted to do? Run your mouth? I'm here now so do what you need to do."

"I'm not going to do anything to you. As we know, I can't. I just have a couple presents for you. I have been waiting for years to give you these. Don't you want your gifts?" he asked as a smile spread across his face.

"What gifts?" I asked feeling a little suspicious.

"Well, here is gift number one." That's when one of the people in a cloak walked up. As they took off their hood, it felt like my heart stopped beating.

Chapter 23

"Well, here is gift number one." That's when one of the people in a cloak walked up. As they took off their hood, it felt like my heart stopped beating. Standing in the place of the stranger was not a stranger at all. It was Justin.

"Justin. Wait… how? How is he still alive? Justin, it's me Ebony. Come here." I start walking to him as tears of joy were pouring out my eyes but he didn't even bulge. He just stared at me.

"Justin, don't you remember me?"

"See, brainwashing him can do the trick. I turned Justin into a vampire because you know it's always good to protect family." Venomar said as he smiled at me. Justin turned around and ran back to him, hugging his legs.

"Family? Don't you dare call us family. You are nowhere near being a part of my family and you will never be." I yelled at him as tears of anger poured out of my eyes. That's when the second person in a cloak walked up and they took off their hood. This stranger was dad.

"Dad? What are you doing here? I thought you were on a business trip." He walks up to me and holds both of my shoulders.

"Ebony, how can I explain this to you? Hell, I might as well just say it. I am not who you think I am. I am your father of course but I am also Venomar's father. Venomar is your half-brother."

"You bastard!!! I can't believe you did this to me!" I hear mom yell from behind me. I turned my head to see Sita holding mom back.

"Don't you dare complain Laura. The secret life you thought you hid from me, I knew about the entire time. Why you think I approached you? Because it was love at first sight? Of course not. I knew you carried the line of the original witches and this was my only way of ending it."

"This can't be true." I said under my breath.

"Aw yes, sweetheart. It is true."

"So you're a part of the Nomeds."

"I'm not only a part of it. I am the leader of it." He said as he smiled at me.

"But dad, I love you. Why would you do this to me."

"Because Ebony, I won't be able to do this if I didn't" he said, imitating me. After that, he smirked and stood back beside Venomar.

"You know, Ebony. It's good to know that my sister knows about me. Know you know that some of my blood runs through your veins." Venomar says. That's when I got really angry.

"Also Ebony? You said you love me, right?" Dad said as he walks up to me. I tried to lift my hands to use my powers on him but he pulled down my hand, with super strong strength. I quickly looked up at him.

"What are you?" I asked.

"I, darling, am the one who is going to take your life." After that, I feel a sharp pain in my chest. I look down and see a knife in my chest.

"Daddy." I say softly as I dropped down to the ground. I tried to breathe but every breath I took seem shorter and shorter.

"Ebony!!!" I hear mom's faint voice. I looked over to where Venomar,dad and Justin stood and they were gone. Next thing I know, Jessica, Sita, mom, Logan and Josh and surrounding me with a bright light behind them. Mom and Jessica are crying, with Sita and Josh comforting them. Logan is hovering over me, with a scared look on his face. I feel him take the knife out but my body is so numb, I don't feel any pain.

"Don't die on me, Ebony. Don't die on me! I should have been right beside you like I said" he says as he looked at me, tears pouring out of his eyes. I used all the strength I had to grab his hand and hold it. I looked back up at him and smiled at him. With the little breath I have left, I hear myself say something.

"Logan… I'm sorry." After that, the light became brighter as I feel myself drift away. That's when everything went black as I took my last breath.

Chapter 24

The Next Day: Logan's POV

This would be a nice view that Ebony would love if she was here. Here on the balcony, you can see the ocean below and the seagulls flying towards the sunset. The breeze was also nice here but it was hard to enjoy it when all I can think about is what happened yesterday. All I can remember is Ebony's blood slipping through my fingers as I tried to put pressure on the wound, trying to keep her from bleeding out, yet all that happened was me watching the life leave her beautiful green eyes I love so much. I looked down as this horrible memory popped up in my mind. I felt a tear come out and drop into the ocean. I should have been right beside her but I wasn't. That should be the one dead. I would trade places with Ebony in a minute because she didn't deserve it. But now it's too late. I turned around and walked back into Sita's room. Jessica was standing right next to Laura, hugging her, while Josh, Alina and Sita were standing next to Sita's bed. Lying in the bed is Ebony's beautiful lifeless body. She was dressed in a long, silky gray dress and her hair was out, cascading over the pillows. Her face is as beautiful as usual, yet instead of the rosy red cheeks I was used to seeing whenever she looked at me were not there and I can't see her beautiful green eyes.

I walked over to the bed and cleared my throat.

"Sorry guys. I can I get some alone time real quick?" I asked.

"Of course you can." Alina said as she tried to give me a smile. Before they walked away, Sita stopped in front of me and looked me in my eyes.

"Logan, you know this is not your fault. You know she died a hero."

"Sita." I said as I looked away. She touched my shoulder and sighed before she walked away. I kneeled beside her as I held her hand.

"I am so sorry, Ebony. I should have been right by your side. If I were, it would have been me dead instead of you. Don't worry. I will fight until it kills me to get back at Venomar and your father. They are the ones who do not deserve to live. The blood you shed from them will be taken from their bodies and I will make sure of that. They took a piece of me with them and I will make sure I will take all from them. I love you, Ebony." I said as I kissed her cheek. I stood up, leaned over and kissed her on her lips. As I leaned back up, I looked into her beautiful face and next thing I know, I am staring into her usual beautiful green eyes. She smiled up at me.

"Count me in."

Made in the USA
Middletown, DE
10 December 2014